THE REMITTANCE MAN

Accused of a murder he didn't commit, Daniel Naughton escapes from jail. He is joined by Lee Pemberton, whose employer has been robbed and shot by the real killers. Lee persuades Daniel that the only way to prove his innocence is to pin down the men responsible. The trail takes them to Los Santos where the Forrester gang rules with fists and guns. But would Daniel and Lee stay alive long enough to bring the killers to justice?

Books by Steven Gray
in the Linford Western Library:

DEATH COMES TO ROCK SPRINGS

STEVEN GRAY

THE REMITTANCE MAN

Complete and Unabridged

LINFORD
Leicester

First published in Great Britain in 1997 by
Robert Hale Limited
London

First Linford Edition
published 1998
by arrangement with
Robert Hale Limited
London

British Library CIP Data

Gray, Steven
    The remittance man.—Large print ed.—
Linford western library
    1. Western stories
    2. Large type books
    I. Title
823.9'14 [F]

ISBN 0–7089–5192–9

Published by
F. A. Thorpe (Publishing) Ltd.
Anstey, Leicestershire

Set by Words & Graphics Ltd.
Anstey, Leicestershire
Printed and bound in Great Britain by
T. J. International Ltd., Padstow, Cornwall

This book is printed on acid-free paper

1

"**D**ANIEL NAUGHTON. Come along, my good man, you must have my money."

"I told you, I've already looked."

"Then look again!"

"I'm sorry, sir . . . "

"Try the Right Honourable Daniel Cedric Arthur Phipps-Naughton." Daniel used his title and full name in case it made a difference to the man's incompetence. It didn't. He glared at the bank clerk who stared back, seeming not at all disturbed that he was annoying such an important person as Daniel, nor at the turmoil in Daniel's chest.

The money had to be here. His father couldn't have forgotten to send it. But, horrors, supposing he wasn't going to provide a remittance for his youngest son — the black sheep of the family — any longer? What would he do then?

"I made all the necessary arrangements to have it transferred here." Daniel tried to keep the tremor from his voice.

"It hasn't arrived yet."

"I demand to see the manager."

"Son, I am the manager."

Daniel sighed heavily. How typical, he sneered. Even in England's smallest hamlet, you wouldn't find the person in charge actually doing the work. That was the trouble with these Westerners, they had no pride.

Daniel always tried to keep the pride in his own bearing, which was sometimes a bit difficult, especially when he was begging, like now. "When do you think it will be here?"

"Try tomorrow, son. Now, if there's nothing more perhaps you'd like to let me get on with my work. I am busy."

Pointedly Daniel looked round. Besides himself, the bank had only one other customer, a farmer's wife, rake-thin and sunburned. "Oh yes, I can see that. Well, I wouldn't want to make you work too hard. You're obviously not used to it."

"And you," the woman said as he stalked by her, "are a very rude young man." And she poked him with her parasol.

As he stepped out into the searing sunlight, Daniel wondered, not for the first time, what he was doing here — not just in America but in New Mexico. Amongst all the greys and browns? The dust, the heat and the discomfort? He should be lounging in the luxury of the Phipps-Naughton manorhouse in Kent, with servants to cater to his every whim.

But if he'd stayed in England he wouldn't be in the Kentish manorhouse, he'd be with his stern grandfather in Scotland; where most certainly he wouldn't be enjoying himself and no one would be catering to even one of his wishes, let alone all of them. It had been either that or come to America and collect a monthly remittance by promising to stay away from England.

As far as Daniel was concerned, he had had no choice.

The trouble was his last remittance had almost been spent and the next hadn't yet arrived.

Daniel was twenty-three. He was tall, with long legs, and wirily lean. He had deep brown eyes and, since arriving in the West, his dark brown hair had grown quite long. He had also taken to wearing Western style clothes — jeans, shirt, vest and boots not only because they were more comfortable but his English suits and shoes had made him an object of derision. He also carried a gun at his side. He hadn't yet found the occasion to fire it, even though some of the people who inhabited the frontier had annoyed him enough that he'd like to have shot them; the trouble was they looked the type who would shoot back.

Juniper City. Daniel surveyed it snootily. How could this place be called a city! It certainly wasn't much like London! Just a couple of banks — he'd already tried the other one in case the arrangements had been muddled — the marshal's office, a stagecoach stop, several stores. And a redlight district that at least hadn't yet been shunted off to the town's outskirts.

He leant against the rail outside the bank and reached into his pockets to count his money. Two dollars, forty-nine cents. Just about enough to have something to eat and then spend the evening gambling; as a result of which he could either get a room in the hotel or be forced to sleep in the livery stable.

If his father could only see him in this awful place and in this situation surely he would regret his decision to send his son into the barren wilderness of America. But maybe not. Because if Daniel was a disappointment to his father then surely his father was a disappointment to Daniel.

The saloon was crowded. It amazed Daniel that no matter where a saloon was situated — a town like Denver, a small place like Juniper City, or in the middle of nowhere — it always was crowded. Where did all the people come from?

Although it still had sawdust on the floor and spittoons by each table, the place had pretensions of glamour — with wooden doors, glass in their upper portions, fancy lettering on the windows, a bar made of mahogany and the glitter of bottles and clean glasses. Tables and chairs were placed all round the floor with some booths lining one wall. A staircase swept upstairs leading to a long corridor off of which were rooms where the few girls wandering amongst the crowd slept with their customers.

Daniel badly wanted to enjoy one of the girls, who, on the whole, looked reasonably young and pretty, but unless he had luck playing cards he wouldn't be able to afford one. However handsome and wonderful he was, these girls wouldn't hand out their favours for anything other than cold hard cash.

There were several card games in progress and a roulette wheel in one corner. After buying himself a beer, and clutching his last dollar, he went over to a table where a poker game was in progress and where, he was pleased to see, none of the other four players had much more than nickels and dimes in front of him.

"Mind if I join in?" he asked when the hand finished.

The four men looked up. One appeared to be a store clerk, two were young cowboys, but the fourth was older, about sixty, with grey hair and beard to match, and well dressed. He also had the most money in front of him.

"Sure," the man said. "You English?"

"Yes, sir. Daniel Naughton." While

being a Right Honourable impressed the gullible, Daniel had mostly given up using both it and his full name. It had just caused confusion and he'd ended up being called 'Mr Phipps' or 'Sir Naughton'.

"And you've come here to Juniper City from all that way away?"

Daniel nodded. He had no intention of telling anyone who didn't need to know that he was a Remittance Man. It was so degrading.

Luckily one of the cowboys had already shuffled the cards and was now dealing them and conversation, except about the game, ceased.

Daniel considered poker, unlike whist or bridge, a game that needed no skills, except a good memory and the ability to bluff. However, money could be won, or lost, quite quickly.

That evening, he lost a few games but won more. While the money in front of him didn't amount to a great deal, it did look as if he'd be able to afford one of the prostitutes, maybe spend the night with her.

In between hands he learned that the man's name was Vincent Ford and that he was a rancher.

"I own the Rocking V about five miles out of town," he explained. "These two young men are my ranchhands. I've got over three hundred head of cattle and I'm hoping to expand. It's a good life."

God, Daniel thought trying not to yawn, if he thought that was a good life he'd never been to London; nor even New York. Where were the lights, the entertainment, the beautiful women?

"Are you going to bet on that hand?" Ford interrupted Daniel's gloomy thoughts. "Or are you going to fold?"

Daniel stared at him weighing up the situation. He and Ford were the only two left in the round; the other three had dropped out. He had put three dollars in the pot and had almost seven in front of him. He could easily fold and still come out with much more than he started with. But . . . he had a good hand — two pair, two tens and two eights. And Ford wasn't a good player, having lost most of the money he'd started out with.

Rashness instead of commonsense won, as it usually did with Daniel.

"I'll see you and raise you two dollars more."

Unfortunately Ford didn't crumble as he was meant to. He raised the stake again. Daniel swallowed. Down to just three dollars if he accepted the bet but he couldn't back out now. Pride and foolishness wouldn't let him. Anyway he was bound to win and look at the amount of money he'd have then!

"I'll see you, Mr Ford. And raise you three more collars." All he had left.

"Are you sure?"

"Yes."

"All right, then. What have you got?"

"Two pair. Tens and eights. Quite good, don't you think, old boy?"

"Yeah. But not quite good enough." And Ford turned over his cards revealing four sixes. "My hand, sir."

Daniel stared at the man, stared at the cards, stared at the money which Ford was pocketing, then grimaced at the few dimes he was left with. "No!" he whispered appalled. He'd lost everything he had.

He looked at Ford again. The rancher was smiling, leaning back in his chair, preparing to light a cigar.

Daniel's face reddened and his quick temper something else responsible for his position — rose up within him.

"You cheat! You bloody goddamned cheat!" he yelled with a colourful mixture of English and American swearwords.

Everything went quiet. The men at his table gaped at him while others craned their necks to see what was happening.

"That's my money!" Daniel cried. Leaping to his feet he scrambled across the tabletop, knocking aside everything in his way, and launched himself at Ford.

They went down in a tangle of arms and legs, the short plump rancher outclassed but determined to give a good account of himself.

A girl screamed, there were cries and yells.

"Hey now!" Someone shouted and hands grabbed at Daniel, pulling him off Ford, separating them, dragging him up.

Yelling "Let me at him," Daniel struggled for a moment, before someone stepped in front of him.

He was a tall man, plump round the middle with balding brown hair, thick sideburns and dark eyes.

His looks didn't really matter. What did matter was that he was the town marshal and that he held a pistol, the barrel of which was stuck in Daniel's chest. And there was a look in the man's eyes that said he wouldn't hesitate to shoot.

2

DANIEL gulped and mumbled, "Don't please." He was aware of the saloon's inhabitants crowding round, nudging one another, grinning. Oh God, he was at the centre of a scene — how embarrassing!

Marshal Jim McCullum nodded to the rancher who was brushing himself down. "Mr Ford," he said then added, "Craig, Johnny," to the two cowboys holding Daniel.

Daniel sighed. The Marshal knew all three men. Not only were the cards stacked against him but so was everything else.

"Mind telling me what's going on here?"

Ford gave a shakey laugh. "Mr Naughton accused me of cheating."

"He did cheat!"

"Then he attacked me."

13

McCullum grinned. "Now, son, why do you think someone like Mr Ford, who owns his own ranch, and certainly doesn't need the money, seeing as how he's almighty generous and is always giving to charitable causes . . . "

Oh bloody hell, Daniel moaned.

" . . . would want to cheat someone like you out of, how much?"

"Seven dollars," Daniel replied sulkily.

"Seven dollars. Mind telling me that?"

"If anyone was cheating it was him," the cowboy called Craig said. He had fair hair and a fair moustache and blue eyes that were extremely angry at the moment.

Daniel pulled himself up straight and stated, not altogether truthfully, "Excuse me, my good man, but I have never cheated when playing cards. I've never needed to."

"You know, son, you sound like you're full of hot air," McCullum said, making everyone laugh. Daniel reddened angrily. "I've been keeping an eye on you since you arrived in town yesterday. You struck me right off as a very strange young man. It seems as if I was right. Not only did you cause a scene at the bank and nearly give Mrs Cummings an attack of the nerves . . . "

"I most certainly did not!" Daniel interrupted indignantly, remembering the way she'd poked him with her parasol; old biddy.

"But now you're fighting in the saloon. Perhaps, son, a night in the cells will calm you down."

"Oh, now, wait a minute."

"Come on, son, and let me have your gun. Don't want you accidentally shooting anyone with it. Not even yourself."

"Do you know who I am?"

"No." And McCullum sounded as if he didn't particularly care.

"I'm the Right Honourable Daniel . . . "

But Daniel's words were lost as the Marshal caught his arm and marched him out of the saloon. As the doors

15

closed behind them the men and the girls went back to whatever they were doing before the excitement broke out.

"Here." Craig Weaver handed Vincent Ford his hat, which had been lost in the struggle. "Are you OK, sir?"

"Yes, thanks to the pair of you. That young idiot! I thought Englishmen were meant to be gentlemen not thugs! Oh well," the man sighed, "it's over now. And I'd better head back for the ranch. Are you two coming or do you want to stay here?"

"We'll go with you." Craig glanced at Johnny Ashbrook. Both of them had hoped to stay overnight in Juniper City but they were fond of the man they worked for and neither liked the thought of him going all the way back to the ranch on his own after what had happened. He was no longer a young man and it was a dark and lonely journey.

"Ain't you going to swear out a complaint against him?" Johnny asked.

Ford shook his head. "It's not worth

it. It's a long time since I was in a fight and I can't say I enjoyed it, but I'm not hurt. Naughton is just a young hothead and a night in jail should be punishment enough."

★ ★ ★

Daniel complained all the way to the jailhouse until McCullum told him to shut up and clouted him round the head.

Back home, Daniel reflected sadly, he'd never be treated like this. And if he was he'd have someone in higher authority than McCullum to complain to about the man's unreasonable behaviour. Out here small town marshals with nothing better to do than bully those unfortunate enough to be in their grasp were a law unto themselves.

McCullum pushed him inside the office. A lamp stood on one of the two desks lighting the interior with a pale glow, not that there was much to see, the only decorations being Wanted posters pinned to the walls. He opened his desk drawer, pulling out a bunch of keys. One unlocked a door in the far wall. He beckoned Daniel through it.

Beyond were four cells, two on either side of a narrow corridor. McCullum opened the first one and pushed Daniel inside.

"I'll see you in the morning. Try to sleep but if you can't try reflecting on how foolish you've been."

"Try buggering off," Daniel muttered.

McCullum shrugged. "You're the one in jail, son, not me. That entitles me to call you foolish. Goodnight."

And he shut the door leaving Daniel in darkness, except for the small square of dull grey light coming in through a barred window at the end of the corridor. Gradually as his eyes became accustomed to the dark, he realized that the cell opposite had an occupant. He could just make out the shape of a body lying under a blanket. Whoever it was hadn't stirred.

Left with no choice but to go to

18

sleep, Daniel lay down on the hard cot, the mattress so thin he could feel the wooden slats underneath it, and pulled an equally thin blanket over him. He rolled over facing the wall.

Oh how glad he was that none of his family could see him — a Right Honourable with a noble name who had once lived in a stately manorhouse locked up in a squalid New Mexican jail cell — what a come down!

* * *

Daniel woke up the following morning surprised he had fallen asleep. His whole body ached from the hard bed. Feeling dirty and thirsty, he sat up and saw that the other prisoner was standing at the bars looking across at him.

He was a young man in his late twenties. Not quite as tall as Daniel but broader and well muscled. He had fair curly hair. His eyes were brown and his skin so tanned he had to work out in the open.

"Hi," he said with the Western informality that always made Daniel grimace in distaste. "What's the Marshal got you in here for?"

"It was a mistake. An extremely bad mistake on someone's part."

The other man grinned. "Name's Lee Pemberton."

Why, oh why, did Westerners never feel the need to wait for formal introductions? Daniel could be quite rude when he wanted and might well not have said anything in return. But at the moment, seeing as he was in a jail cell, he decided he had no real justification for feeling superior. "Daniel Naughton." He felt sure the man opposite would never understand the finer points of a double-barrelled surname.

"Well, if you're going to be in here for a while the Marshal ain't too bad and the food's pretty good."

Daniel looked horrified. "I jolly well

hope I'm not kept in here. I ought to be let go at once. It was all a misunderstanding."

"Your accent's strange. Where you from? New York?"

Daniel, who could well have said something scathing about the other man's drawl being strange too, said, "No, my good man, I'm from England."

"You're a long way from home."

"Yes," Daniel agreed sadly. "A very long way."

At that moment the door to the office opened and the Marshal came in.

"All right, Mr Naughton, you can leave now."

"I can?" Daniel was surprised. Despite his protestations of outraged innocence, he knew he'd been in the wrong and was sure he'd be appearing before whatever sort of judge Juniper City had.

"Yeah. You're lucky. Mr Ford has decided not to press charges against you. And I've been over to the bank.

21

Your remittance is in so you won't have any more money worries."

"Oh really!" Daniel muttered, turning to pick up his coat and hat. Did the Marshal have to tell everyone about his financial circumstances?

Not that Pemberton was taking much notice, he was obviously more concerned about his stomach because he said, "Hey, Marshal, where's my breakfast? I'm hungry."

McCullum grinned. "Don't worry, Lee, it'll be along in a minute. Bacon, beans, biscuits and good strong coffee."

Lee looked pleased while Daniel shuddered. Hadn't they ever heard of tea, toast and scrambled eggs?

In the office McCullum handed over the gun he'd taken from Daniel the previous night.

"Go and get your money. Have something to eat. And if you feel like staying in Juniper City you'll be welcome so long as you behave yourself."

"Oh don't worry, Marshal," Daniel

said extremely haughtily. "I only came to your town to collect my money. And nothing but absolutely nothing would induce me to stay here a moment longer than is strictly necessary!"

At last he could be on his way to Arizona and the fortune he hoped to make there.

3

IT was a fine morning, the heat made bearable by a cool breeze. The meadow, as well as the high ridge towards which Daniel was riding, was covered with blue and yellow flowers, the grass still green and lush.

He felt almost happy. Until he heard the sounds of shots.

Daniel pulled his horse to a halt. The firing came from beyond the ridge. Should he investigate or wait where he was?

This would never have happened in England. Of course thieves and roadside robbers existed there — armed ones too — but more usually they carried knives and sticks, they rarely had guns. Here it seemed everyone owned guns and weren't reluctant to use them. If he rode over the ridge he could be struck by a stray bullet.

And there were wild Indians to worry about too. You certainly didn't find them riding around the Kentish countryside! Daniel had no idea which Indians lived in this part of New Mexico but he was quite sure they wouldn't be friendly towards a lone white traveller.

On occasions discretion was definitely a better part of valour; this was one of them. Daniel stayed where he was until his dilemma was solved for him and the shooting stopped as suddenly as it had started.

Cautiously he urged his horse to the top of the hill and there came to another halt.

In the wide valley below was a ranchhouse surrounded by barns and corrals, in one of which some horses milled. A few cattle grazed round a nearby waterhole. Otherwise the place was deserted with no sign of life . . .

No, wait, there! Another small range of hills encroached on the valley's far side and riding up the first slope were four men. At least, Daniel sighed in some relief, they were riding away in the opposite direction and luckily they weren't Indians belonging to a warparty! As he watched they rode over the top of the hill and disappeared from view.

The next question was whether or not he should ride down to the ranchhouse and see what had happened. He didn't want to. He wanted to ride away and have nothing more to do with it. But supposing someone was shot, hurt, and needed help?

"Oh damn," he said out loud as his conscience got the better of him. He urged his horse into a trot and rode down the hill.

He dismounted in the yard before the house. Daniel didn't know much about ranches — and didn't want to learn — but this place had a prosperous look about it. The house was quite large with a porch running all the way round it and glass in the windows, the barns and the corrals were in good repair and the horses looked sleek and well fed.

"Hallo," he called.

No reply.

"Is anyone here? Hallo." Feeling a bit foolish Daniel drew his gun, holding it down by his side, hardly able to believe he was behaving in such a way. He might have to shoot someone; worse he could get himself shot. But although he wanted to turn and run away he walked slowly towards the house, stepping up onto the porch. The front door was open. He paused by it, calling out again but still received no reply.

He should leave while he could. Instead he went into the house, finding himself in the main parlour. It was wrecked. The furniture was tipped over, paper spilled onto the floor, glass broken underfoot.

And, in the middle of the wreckage, sprawled on his back, sightless eyes staring up at the ceiling, a large hole gaping in his chest, was Vincent Ford.

"Oh my God," Daniel whispered, fighting down sickness.

He'd never seen a dead body before but there was absolutely no doubt that Ford was dead.

He took a quick backwards step towards the door.

And heard a scuffling sound behind him. The robbers had come back and would kill him as well! His heart skipped several frightened beats. But before he could do anything, before he could even turn round, hands grasped him round the shoulders and he was pulled off his feet and thrown from the porch. He landed on the ground so hard he bounced, his grip on his gun lost.

Even as he struggled to sit up someone cried out, "Mr Ford is dead! The bastard shot him!"

And he looked up to see the two cowboys who had sat in on the poker game. What were their names? Craig and Johnny.

"You bastard!" That was the one

called Craig, the one who had flung him to the ground. The hothead. He jumped down and kicked out, catching Daniel hard in the thigh.

Daniel rolled away. "Wait a minute!" he protested. "I didn't do anything!"

"Do you deny Mr Ford is in there, in his own house, shot to death?" Johnny yelled.

"No. But I didn't do it. There were four other men . . . "

"Oh yeah?" Craig sneered. "When we heard the shots we came hotfoot from the far end of the meadow. We didn't see anyone."

"They rode into the hills."

"You came out here to rob Mr Ford because he beat you at cards." Craig kicked Daniel again.

"Ow! Stop that! I'm innocent." Somehow Daniel managed to scramble to his feet. He was very scared. He was faced by two angry young men who were convinced he'd just killed their employer. And he could see how bad it looked for him. He was in the house with the dead rancher, he'd had his gun out and these idiots hadn't seen the men responsible.

They could hit him. They could hurt him. He'd never be able to defend himself. Daniel wasn't much good at fist fighting. They might even shoot him. What should he do? Beg, cry? Assume a superior manner? Yes, that would impress them.

"Why should I shoot someone for a paltry seven dollars? I have money of my own. I'm an important gentleman and gentlemen don't go around shooting other gentlemen."

Unfortunately Daniel didn't think he sounded very superior. He sounded frightened. And equally unfortunately the two cowboys weren't in the least bit impressed. Instead they gaped at one another as if they had no idea what he was talking about.

Johnny said, "Oh, lock the silly bastard up in the store room, while I go and fetch the Marshal."

At least they weren't going to shoot

him out of hand. Marshal McCullum had struck Daniel as a fairly decent sort, even if not particularly intelligent. He would recognize the truth when he heard it.

★ ★ ★

"So," Marshal McCullum said when Craig hauled Daniel from the store room, "you decided not only to rob Mr Ford but to kill him as well."

"No!" Daniel looked at the lawman in some exasperation and took back his earlier appraisal of him. He wasn't in the least bit intelligent! "For goodness sake, my good man, I'm innocent. Surely you can see that."

"All I can see is a dead man, shot and killed and robbed in his own home. A man that only last night you threatened and actually attacked. And now here you are found bending over his body."

"I told you. There were four other men . . . "

"Men no one else saw."

"That's right, Marshal," Craig put in. "The only one we saw was this bastard."

"You're under arrest." McCullum nodded at the very young deputy who had accompanied him. "Adam, handcuff him and we'll take him in."

"No, wait, listen," Daniel protested. "If I robbed Mr Ford then where's the money? You can search me if you like and you won't find anything except my remittance."

"Look, son, I think you're quick tempered and stupid with it but not that stupid. You've obviously hidden it."

"Why should I do that?"

"So you can say exactly what you have."

"Then where is it?" Daniel spread his arms. "Besides I wouldn't have had time to hide it."

"Sure you would," Craig said. "It was some time before Johnny and I got here."

"Why should I?" Daniel repeated. "Why not just ride away with it?"

"Because you wanted to see what else you could steal."

"Oh, really! Look if you can accept that you took so long to get here that I'd have time to do all these terrible things, why can't you believe that you took long enough for the real killers to ride away?"

"We weren't that goddamned long!"

McCullum said, "We can sort this out later on. Right now let's be on our way."

"Well, Marshal, you might not think I'm stupid but I sure as hell think you are!"

"Sonofabitch! Mr Ford was a friend and I don't like cocky know-it-alls."

And McCullum promptly showed Daniel how much he didn't like him by hitting him hard in the stomach. As Daniel doubled up, gasping for breath, he was punched and knocked down.

"Just so as you remember who's in

charge," McCullum said, kicking him once or twice.

Daniel curled up in a ball, aware of the other three watching and knowing they wouldn't do anything to help him. That they were enjoying seeing him being beaten up. He began to whimper. This hurt! But his torment didn't last long. McCullum wasn't a deliberately cruel man. He just wanted to make sure his prisoner didn't give him any trouble.

He dragged Daniel up and said, "You really ain't up to much are you?"

Which didn't exactly make Daniel feel any better.

And he certainly felt much worse when, with his hands cuffed behind him, he was taken back to Juniper City.

And for the second time in two days he found himself locked up in the town jail; this time for the much more serious crime of murder.

4

NO sooner had the cell door clanged shut on Daniel than the Marshal opened the one where Lee Pemberton stood watching curiously.

"OK, Lee, you're free to go."

"I am?"

"Yeah."

"But there's a couple more days of my sentence still to go."

"Don't worry 'bout that. I'll square it with the judge. Do you wanna go or not?"

Pemberton shrugged and followed the Marshal. At the door to the office he glanced back over his shoulder at Daniel, a worried frown on his face.

Daniel's heart sank. Why had the Marshal let his other prisoner go? There could be only one reason. Vincent Ford had evidently been popular with and generous to the citizens of Juniper City. Once the news of his shooting and the arrest of his murderer was spread, the townsmen would gather together, get drunk and angry, and form a lynchmob. Probably led by those two cowboys who worked at the ranch. And Marshal McCullum didn't want a witness to the fact that he was going to hand Daniel over to them without even pretending to put up a fight to protect him.

His knees giving way, Daniel sat down on the bunk, head in his hands. If only, only, frontiersmen weren't so ready to indulge in violence and were instead willing to listen to reason.

Apart from the young deputy who brought him some stew and coffee, he was left alone. The deputy didn't answer any of his questions about what was happening but stared at him as if he was scared that the prisoner was some sort of monster.

As night fell Daniel could hear a lot of noise from outside — shouts, yells, horses galloping up and down. As he'd been asleep the previous night he had no way of knowing if Juniper City was normally like this. But he doubted it. This was the mob getting itself worked up and he wondered what time the men would come for him. They'd have to drink quite a lot first to get both their courage and their anger stoked up. About midnight he decided.

He stared at his watch. 9 o'clock. He had three more hours to live. Then the mob would storm the jail and McCullum would not only stand aside, he might even give them the key to the cell. What would happen then? Would the good citizens also take the opportunity to kick and punch him, or would they be content to just hang him?

And how would he behave? In the dime novels he'd read where a lynching had taken place the victim, if the villain, had sneered to the last; if the hero, he'd been calm and brave until rescued at the last minute by the virginal heroine.

In this, his darkest hour, Daniel admitted to himself that he was neither villain nor hero and he certainly wasn't very brave. He would probably scream for mercy, weep and shake; all of which would provide his tormentors with a good laugh but would hardly lessen their resolve. Unfortunately there was no heroine, virginal or otherwise, to put in a good word for him.

It wouldn't be so bad — but he was innocent. He hadn't done anything. It wasn't fair. Oh why, why hadn't he ridden on? Why had he done the right thing?

The door banged open. Startled, scared, Daniel leapt to his feet.

It was McCullum. "Just thought I'd look in on you to see you was OK before I went home for the night."

"Please, Marshal, don't do this. Don't go."

"I'll be back in the morning."

Yes — when it would be too late.

"Deputy Fox will be here to look after you."

"At least let me have a pen and piece of paper so that I can write to my father and tell him my sad story." Daniel wanted to make sure that his father knew he was responsible, and was sorry, for his son's death; that he realized it was his fault for sending him to America in the first place.

"There'll be plenty of time for that later on."

"Really, when?"

"In the next few days while you're waiting for a fair trial."

Oh, ha! Bloody ha! Daniel thought.

"Don't fret, son, you might even be sentenced to a prison term instead of hanging. It all depends on what mood the judge is in and what sort of tale you can come up with to explain what you did. But no one likes cold blooded murder so I expect it'll be a hanging.

"Night, son, sleep tight."

Daniel refused to answer and turned his back on the man. This was awful.

He didn't want to die. Especially here in Juniper City, New Mexico, of all terrible places. "Oh, please, please, someone help me," he said out loud. But he didn't expect anyone to answer him; and no one did.

For the next hour Daniel paced the small cell or sat on the bunk sunk in despair.

11 o'clock. He was sure the sounds from outside were growing louder by the minute. He might not even have until midnight. The lynchmob could be coming for him any moment.

He had to do something. He couldn't just sit waiting to be lynched. But what?

"Deputy! Hey, deputy!"

At first Daniel didn't think the young man was going to take any notice. Then slowly the door opened and Adam Fox put his head round it.

"What do you want?"

"Some water. Can I have a glass of water?"

"I don't know. The Marshal didn't

say anything 'bout that."

"What harm can it do? My throat is parched dry. Come along, my dear chap, what have you got to be frightened of? I'm locked up. You can pass me the glass through the bars. What can I do?"

Adam Fox looked at him hesitantly, at last saying, "All right."

Daniel waited impatiently for his return. He had no idea what he was going to do; or if he was even going to attempt to do anything.

Fox soon reappeared with a glass of water. "Stand back."

Daniel stepped away from the cell door. Fox put the glass on one of the vertical bars and Daniel yelled, "Watch out!"

Fox was already jumpy and at the shout he let go of the glass. Daniel leapt forward, grabbed it before it fell and flung it and its contents at the deputy. Fox staggered backwards, holding his hands up in front of his face. Daniel caught his arm, holding it tight. He reached through with his other hand tugging at Fox's hair, banging the deputy's head against the bars.

Fox yelped in pain and tried to struggle away. Somehow Daniel got hold of the man's gun, jerking it from its holster. He bashed Fox on the side of the head. Fox's eyes glazed over and he crumpled to the floor in an untidy heap.

"And now what?" Daniel thought. He stared down at the deputy's inert body. Fox wasn't carrying the keys to the cell and there was no way he would go and fetch them just because Daniel had the gun. All he'd have to do was go into the office and shut the door behind him. Daniel couldn't do anything then. All he'd succeeded in doing was putting himself in more trouble, unless . . .

He had no choice but to shoot out the lock. Someone might hear but then again they were making so much noise outside that that was unlikely. And if Juniper City was like a lot of other frontier towns he'd passed through, shots were commonplace and no one took much notice of them.

It was worth the risk.

He placed the barrel of the gun against the lock, turned away and fired. The shot sounded very loud in the confined space of the cells. And nothing had happened. But with the second blast the lock shattered and the cell door swung open.

Daniel made sure that the deputy wasn't badly hurt — he felt bad about hitting him like that — after all he'd just been doing his job and had been left in the office on his own to take the blame for whatever happened to the prisoner. He then went into the office and collected his gun, flinging the belt over his shoulder. He opened the door, quite sure the Marshal or the lynchmob would be on the other side arriving to investigate the two shots. He was wrong.

Quite a crowd had gathered outside the saloon but that was way off down the road. Obviously they hadn't heard anything.

Keeping to the shadows, he crept along the side of the building, heading for the livery stable where presumably the Marshal had left his horse. All the way his heart was in his mouth fearing a shout of discovery or the deputy raising the alarm. He should have locked Fox up in one of the cells but he couldn't take the time to go back now. He felt a bit safer when he reached the corner and left the main street and the redlight district behind. Here in the business district all was in darkness with no lamps and no lights shining in any of the buildings.

The door to the stables was open and the owner snoring in a bed of straw in one corner. Several horses stood in the stalls and Daniel was relieved to see his animal. He didn't particularly want to add horsetheft to his list of crimes. That really would be a hanging offence!

With trembling hands he saddled

and bridled the horse, patting it in the hope it wouldn't make any noise and waken the stableman. He made sure the rifle was in its scabbard and that his canteen and saddlebags were there as well.

He led the horse to the stable door and out into the street. All was still dark and quiet. He mounted and then his fear having risen with every passing moment he abandoned all caution and dug heels into the animal's sides, urging it into a gallop.

Bent low over the saddle he fled the town, expecting the sounds of pursuit. But there were none. He was free and clear.

5

OR maybe not.

After riding for a couple of hours through the night, Daniel, weary and aching a bit from the beating McCullum had given him, found a place to stop. It was in the middle of a stand of rocks where neither he nor his horse could be seen from the plains below. He tied the animal to a stunted bush, curled up in his saddle blanket and was almost at once fast asleep.

The next morning when he stirred and woke up, Lee Pemberton sat across from him, holding his gun idly but ready.

"Bloody hell!" Daniel exclaimed, sitting up straight.

"Hi. The last time I saw you I felt sure you were going to end up swinging on a rope."

"So did I," Daniel managed to say when he'd got his breath back.

"Don't tell me the Marshal let you go, especially when he had you dead to rights for shooting one of his citizens."

"No he didn't. Neither did I. Shoot anyone that is."

"So what happened? How come you're out here and not still in jail?"

"I escaped."

"How?"

"I knocked the deputy out. Are you going to take me back?"

"Give me one good reason why I shouldn't."

"I'm innocent. I didn't do anything."

"That's what everyone says. Hell, I even said it myself. But the Judge didn't believe me. Why should I believe you?"

"Because if I'd shot Mr Ford for his money, where is it now? Why did I stay around waiting to be caught? And besides I saw the four men who did it."

Lee sat up straighter. "Four men?"

"That's right. I heard them shooting then I saw them riding away. Trouble is no one believes me."

"I do."

* * *

"I'm sorry, Marshal, real sorry," Adam Fox kept saying. "He tricked me." The young man sat in the marshal's office, a bandage round his head and several bruises on his face. "I shoulda been more careful."

McCullum patted his arm. "Don't worry. It wasn't your fault." He tried to sound calm but inside he was furious. He didn't like losing prisoners, especially ones like Daniel Naughton. He'd been thinking that maybe Naughton was innocent but now, by escaping, he'd sealed his guilt in the Marshal's eyes. But his escape wasn't Adam's fault. The boy was young and inexperienced and McCullum shouldn't have left him alone and in charge. It was lucky he didn't have another body on his hands because Naughton could have murdered Adam too.

"Can I come with you?"

"No. Don't worry, Adam," he added because the boy looked upset, "it ain't because I'm mad at you but you're hurt. You heard what the doctor said. You need to rest. And it ain't like I ain't got enough volunteers." He patted the deputy's arm again, picked up his rifle making sure it was loaded, and went outside.

He was right. Ten or more men waited for him, already mounted, McCullum's horse with them. Other men and women lined the streets to send the posse on its way. In front of the men were the two cowboys, Craig Weaver and Johnny Ashbrook. They both looked grim and determined.

As McCullum swung up onto his horse's back, Craig urged, "Let's go get the sonofabitch."

"I don't want any trouble." McCullum pointed a finger at him.

"You won't get it from me," Craig said sulkily.

"Just remember," McCullum warned them all, "you're my legal deputies. You've sworn oaths to uphold the law. That means that unless there's no other choice we try to get Naughton to surrender and we bring him back here alive and able to stand trial. There'll be no shooting out of hand and no talk of punishing him." He eyed the men sternly. "Do you understand?"

"Yes, Marshal," they chorused.

"Let's go then." McCullum rode to the head of the posse and followed by the cheers of the gathered townspeople they rode out of Juniper City. He didn't think it would take them long or be very difficult to catch up with Daniel Naughton.

* * *

"Here." Lee handed Daniel a cup of hot, strong coffee.

Longing for a cup of tea, Daniel

sipped at it. "Why do you believe me?"

"Because I'm after the same four men."

"You are?"

"Yeah. I come from Texas where I'm a foreman on a large ranch down in the Big Bend country. A couple of weeks ago I was with my boss when he sold some cattle up in Sante Fe, for one of the Indian Reservations. After a good time in one or two of the saloons we headed back home."

"But you never got there?"

"No." Lee's face darkened in remembrance. "We were about thirty miles from Juniper City when one night four men approached our camp. I was a bit suspicious of them but Mr Rice offered them hospitality. They were a father and three sons. Said they were on a cattle buying trip. Yeah, other people's cattle with other people's money!"

"They robbed you?"

"Not only that but when Mr Rice

protested they drew their guns. Mr Rice was shot and killed and they grazed me." Lee put down his coffee and opened his shirt to reveal a livid new scar across his chest. "I guess they thought I was dead too or that I wasn't important enough to worry about. Anyway they left me there on the ground. And when I came to they'd gone, so had our horses and all the money."

"What did you do?"

Lee looked at Daniel as if there was only one answer to that and Daniel should have known what it was. "I set out to find the gang, recover the money and avenge Mr Rice. He was a good employer. He didn't deserve to die like that."

Daniel didn't bother to ask why Pemberton hadn't gone to the law. Frontiersmen seemed to like to take the law into their own hands. "And you followed them as far as Juniper City?"

"Yeah. But it took me a while

because I was on foot. Once I got there I sent a telegraph to the boys at the ranch to let them know what had happened. And then I had to do a couple of days work."

"Why?"

"They'd taken all my money. I had to get some more to buy a horse and supplies."

"Oh, yes, I see. But how did you end up in jail?"

Lee reddened and lowered his eyes. "I got a job as a swamper in one of the saloons. One night I had too much to drink and got in a fight. While I admit I was always fighting in my youth, Mr Rice cured me of my wild ways. I was real ashamed of myself. I suppose my only excuse was still being upset from seeing Mr Rice gunned down. It was stupid. Those bastards were already a long way ahead of me, and because I'd acted so foolishly I thought I'd let them get away. Now it seems that they're still in the area and I've got a chance to catch up with 'em again."

He drained the last of his coffee and stood up, going over to his horse. He glanced at Daniel. "Well ain't you coming?"

Daniel gaped at him. "No, why should I?" He'd been going to ride as far and as fast from Juniper City as he possibly could. Chasing a cut-throat gang instead of escaping didn't appeal much.

"Well, you don't want to be forever looking over your shoulder, do you? You already know that if you're caught you'll be hung iffen, after your escape from jail, you ain't shot as soon as the law sets eyes on you. And it seems to me you'll be easy for the law to trace."

"How?"

"Because you have to give your rightful name each month when you go to pick up your remittance."

"Oh, oh yes." Daniel had forgotten the other man knew about his monetary situation.

"And I guess you can't do without that."

"Er . . . no."

"Have you got any money now?"

"Not much."

"Then you'll need some won't you?"

"I suppose so."

"What were you hoping to do once you got away?"

"I don't know," Daniel had to admit. "I hadn't thought that far ahead."

"What about going back home to England?"

"Umm, maybe." Daniel didn't sound too sure. His father might not want his youngest son to be hung but at the same time he might not accept a wanted murderer in his home.

"Well if you do you'll need money. Which will mean having to give your own name or an address where the money can be sent. Either way you run the risk of being traced."

"I could go back to New York and contact my family from there."

"Don't you think Marshal McCullum will think of that?"

"Surely he won't chase me all that way?"

"He can send out telegraphs warning people to be on the look out for you."

"Do you think he'll bother?"

"Yep. Seems like the only way you're going to prove your innocence is by finding the men who are actually guilty."

Oh dear, Daniel thought, that sounds dangerous.

He didn't want to go up against four outlaws, who would give him even less of a chance than Marshal McCullum, but then again he most certainly didn't want to be hanged. Maybe if he was very lucky he could find proof of the outlaws' guilt without actually confronting them. Or Lee Pemberton could be persuaded to do all the dangerous things — he obviously liked shooting and fighting — while Daniel skulked safely in the rear.

What should he do? What could he do?

"I guess you don't know this area very well?"

Daniel shook his head.

"Nor do I. But I also guess I'm better at finding my way round than you are. You might think you're getting away and really be riding round in a big circle."

"Is that what I've done?" Daniel asked, dismayed.

"You sure have. I think you need me, don't you? And as I'm not going with you, you might as well stick with me and mebbe save your hide at the same time. So if you're coming we oughta get a move on. The posse won't be far behind you. So, what do you say?"

"I haven't got any choice, have I?"

"Not much of a one."

Sighing heavily, Daniel got on his horse. "Where are we going?"

"Back to Mr Ford's ranch. We'll try to pick up the trail there."

6

"SO, Danny, how come you're a remittance man?"

Daniel closed his eyes and gritted his teeth in annoyance. Why did Westerners have to be so informal, especially on such short acquaintance? In England his superiors called him Phipps-Naughton; his friends Naughton; his inferiors sir. Only his family ever called him Daniel. Daniel not Danny. Never Danny. Tell a Westerner his name and he immediately became Danny.

They were also curious and not backward in indulging their curiosity and now Lee was looking at him waiting for an answer.

"Oh, you know," he said airily, "the usual. Drinking. Gambling. Having tradesmen bothering me because I couldn't pay what I owed them.

58

Being so handsome girls always found me irresistible was part of the trouble too. What's the matter?" Daniel added because his companion looked cross.

"Out here we might buy things on tick but it's on the understanding that we pay for them as soon as possible."

"Tradesmen are there for the privileged classes to owe money to. It's accepted. It happens all the time in England."

"That don't make it right. And, Danny, we respect girls."

"So do I," Daniel said a bit sulkily. This wasn't meant to be happening. Others should gasp at his audacity, admire what he'd done, look up to him; not criticize him. "The girls I'm talking of were paid to like me. My father didn't approve."

"He evidently didn't approve or accept your other behaviour either."

"Well, er, no, I suppose not. My last gambling debt was the final straw that broke the back of my father's patience. Especially when the man I owed it to actually came to the door demanding payment. Father said I had to learn my lesson. He gave me an ultimatum. Either go to live with my grandfather in Scotland or go to America." Daniel shook his head. "I'm not sure where he got the idea from. One of his respectable friends I expect."

"How long have you been in America?"

"Almost six months. I landed in New York in January."

"But you didn't stay there?"

"No."

"Why not?"

"It was very expensive there. My remittance hardly went anywhere. And almost as awkward as in England. There was this one man who threatened me because I had four aces, and one of them came from the bottom of the deck. Quite unreasonable. A move seemed the prudent course of action."

"But why out here? To the frontier?" Lee didn't wait for an answer but went on. "Perhaps you like the freedom. The open spaces. The informality."

Daniel looked at him aghast. "You've just mentioned all the things I don't like!"

"Well then perhaps it's something to do with seeing what's over the next hill. I know I used to feel that way till I settled down on Mr Rice's ranch. And there sure are a lot of hills out here. Or maybe it's just an excuse to get into more trouble."

"I can assure you I don't go around looking for trouble."

"No, I know, it just seems to find you! Anyway you've certainly settled in well. You look and act the part . . . "

Daniel didn't know whether to be pleased or angry.

" . . . although once you open your mouth you give yourself away."

"I certainly have no intention of learning how to drawl!" Was Pemberton right? Surely not. Daniel's move out here had been one of economic necessity and the hope of making easy money out of the yokels. Not because he thought he'd like it. Anyway time to put Pemberton in his place. "You know you're quite wrong, I'd go back home at once if only I could. Back to civilisation, comforts, all the things that make life worthwhile. To where some people are recognized as superior to others."

"Like you, you mean?"

Daniel nodded. Of course that was what he meant.

"Why don't you at least go back east then? Washington, maybe. Boston."

"Because, Pemberton, at the moment it simply doesn't suit me to do so."

"The name's Lee."

"I'm an English gentleman, I call other gentlemen by their surnames."

"Why?"

"Because that's what we do. It's polite." Daniel didn't like this cross-examination, it was making him think too hard about his situation. "And really can we change the subject? In England we don't spend all our time wanting to know each other's business."

Lee grinned but didn't say anything about Daniel getting on his high horse. He didn't know whether to believe all he said or not. No doubt he had got into trouble, on more than one occasion, and finally been shown the door by his angry father. But a lot of what he did and said seemed like show, as if that was how he believed Americans would think an English gentleman behaved. He didn't even know if Daniel believed all he said or whether that was show too. It seemed like an exaggerated act; boasting in the hope of making an impression to detract from the fact that he was, actually, a Remittance Man.

*　*　*

Craig Weaver got off his horse and scrambled up amongst the rocks. Someone had lit a fire up here and not long ago.

"Marshal, Naughton's met up with someone else."

"Are you sure?"

"Yeah. There are two sets of footprints, two horses. They reached here at different times, oh a couple of hours apart I should think, had something to eat, then rode out together."

McCullum pushed his hat to the back of his neck and scratched his balding head. Did Naughton know anyone out here or was the meeting a coincidence?

"Can you tell how long ago they left here?"

"Two, three hours."

"Good. That means they ain't too far ahead of us. We ride hard we should soon catch up with 'em."

★ ★ ★

Daniel and Lee had ridden for several hours through the hills, where Daniel had seen the four riders, and then across a valley dotted with rocky outcrops, copses of trees and sagebrush. Apart from a few stray cattle, perhaps belonging to the dead Vincent Ford, they saw no one and nothing, until they came to the foothills on the far side of the valley.

"Look," Lee pointed.

Over against the rocks, sheltered by juniper trees, was a long low building of adobe. An empty corral stood off to one side and there was a well nearby. Smoke spiralled out of a chimney.

The path they were following took them right by the place and as they rode nearer, the door opened. A man appeared in the entrance. He held a rifle.

As Daniel and Lee looked at one another in some surprise, the man yelled, "Hold it right there!" And he raised the gun pointing it at them.

"We don't mean any harm," Lee called back. "Be careful, Danny, don't make any sudden moves."

Daniel had no intention of doing so!

"Come on in then. Slow and steady-like."

The man kept the gun on them all the while they rode up to him and dismounted by the corral.

"We just want some water for our horses and food for ourselves," Lee said.

"So you say. I've already been robbed by those who said much the same."

"Not by four men?" Daniel glanced at Lee.

"Yeah." The man's eyes narrowed. "What do you know about them?"

"We're after 'em for shooting two men aways back."

"Guess I was lucky then. You'd better come on in."

The man introduced himself as Bob Gibson. He made a living out of trading to ranchers and to Indians.

"I've been in the area a long time," he added, putting plates of something that was meant to be beefstew down in front of them.

"And you get on all right with the Indians?" Daniel asked in some surprise.

"Nearly always have an Apache squaw around the place. Ain't got a wife right now but I'm on the look out for one. Anyway you treat the Indians OK they'll do the same to you. They ain't always wanting to take scalps."

Daniel remained unconvinced.

"Perhaps we can buy some provisions while we're here." Lee looked round the store whose shelves, counter and floor were stacked with various kinds of goods; food, furs, farm implements, clothes.

"Still got plenty of goods. Ain't got no money or horses. Bastards took both. Even the poor old mule. Do the pair of you know exactly who it is you're chasing?"

"No," Daniel replied, not liking the sound of that. "Do you?"

"I've heard tales of 'em. The Forrester gang. Father, Bruce, and his three sons, Dirk, Pat and Rex. I was surprised to see 'em this far from the border. They ain't bothered me before and from what I hear they usually congregate down around Arizona and Mexico, raiding into one or the other and then escaping over the opposite border. They hail from a town called Los Santos."

"I think I've heard of that," Lee said.

"Ain't ever been there myself but I hear tell it was once a quite prosperous town. It's over in the Mimbres Mountains."

"And this gang stay there do they?"

"Dunno 'bout that exactly. Just that the town ain't got no law and none likely to go there so that's where they have a good time, buy supplies, that sort of thing."

"Then, Danny, that's where we ought to go."

"Well you two be careful. The Forresters are ruthless and won't hesitate to kill anyone who gets in their way."

Oh dear, Daniel thought, this was sounding worse and worse all the time.

When he'd finished his stew, Lee went around the store buying some tins of food, coffee, sugar and ammunition.

"You ready?" he asked, paying up. "We'd better be on our way."

After what he'd heard, Daniel was thinking of giving up trying to prove his innocence and taking his chances with running away.

He wasn't given the chance.

When they got outside the sounds of shouts and shots suddenly came to them. And as they swung round a group of riders came hurtling along the track towards them.

The posse had caught up!

7

IT was mid-morning and the café was quiet. Those wanting breakfast had gone and the lunchtime diners hadn't yet arrived. Clara Long finished clearing the tables and carried the dirty dishes through to the kitchen where Conchita Delgado, helped by her brother, Miguel, was washing up.

"You finish these," Clara said. "I'll lay the tables for lunch."

"Si, Clara. It won't take long."

Clara smiled. Conchita might be only sixteen but she was a fast, good worker and she would make sure the younger Miguel did his share before being allowed to go home to continue the studying he loved.

Clara began taking the gingham cloths off the tables, shaking them and relaying them. The café had a reputation not only for good food but neat cleanliness too. It meant she was never short of customers.

She was twenty-six, of middle height with a good figure. Her hair was light brown and she kept it pinned back from her face and hanging in waves down her back. She had brown eyes and was nice looking.

She was proud of owning the café — or at least owning the bank's mortgage on it — and was determined to make it a success. It was hard work but worthwhile when she considered her independence and how people in Los Santos thought well of her.

With clean cutlery in her hands she wandered over to one of the windows looking out.

"Oh no!"

"What is matter, Clara?" Conchita came to stand next to her.

Clara didn't answer. She merely nodded towards the other side of the plaza where the four members of the Forrester gang were dismounting from their horses.

The Forrester family was the one drawback to living in Los Santos. They used the town to buy supplies, sometimes paying for what they wanted, sometimes not bothering; and to drink, gamble and whore. Generally cause trouble. And no one was brave or foolhardy enough to go up against them.

"Conchita send Miguel home, now, and you stay in the back, understand?"

"But, Clara . . . "

"I'll be all right. Go on, do as I say."

None of the Forresters liked Mexicans. If they came into the café and found Conchita or Miguel, they were quite likely to beat them up, even though one was a girl and the other a child.

"Please don't let them come in here," Clara prayed to herself. But already Rex Forrester was staring cross at the café. She shuddered.

Bruce Forrester, the father, was in his fifties. A big, burly man with bushy fair hair and a long fair beard. He had cruel light blue eyes, a deep scar over his right one.

The eldest son, Dirk, who was now thirty-two, took after him, with his greasy fair hair and a beard. The younger two, Pat and Rex, were like their mother with dark brown hair and brown eyes. But while Pat was as loutish and lumpish as his brother, Rex's hair was cut short and well combed. He liked to dress well and thought himself a ladies' man.

And the lady he presently wanted was Clara. He couldn't understand why she didn't in turn want him; he didn't believe her. And the more she said no, the more obsessed he became and the more determined to make her say yes.

Clara watched, her heart twisting, as Rex said something to his father and Forrester banged his son on the arm and both Dirk and Pat grinned. She didn't doubt that whatever he'd said was about her. And while they sauntered off in the direction of the nearest saloon, Rex hitched up his trousers, ran a hand through his hair and headed for the café.

Why couldn't he leave her alone? Why not accept she didn't want anything to do with him? She had tried being polite, rude, aggressive. She had pleaded with him. Nothing worked. And while she didn't like to admit it, even to herself, Clara was scared of the young man and what he might do.

* * *

When he saw the Forresters, Alf Perkins hid in his office, hoping no one knew he was there and came in demanding he chase them away.

Perkins was about the nearest thing to a law officer they had in Los Santos. He was the Town Constable. He wasn't very good at his job. He'd only agreed to do it because he thought it would be easy and because, although it didn't pay very well, there were

lots of opportunities to accept bribes
from those who wanted him to turn a
blind eye.

There were other perks to the job.
Free drinks. An hour or two with
a whore now and then. A certain
amount of respect. The latter had
been put in jeopardy by the arrival
of the Forresters. How could anyone
respect him when he hid when they
were in town? And although no one
else was brave enough to do anything
about them they at least had the excuse
it wasn't their job. Well no way was
Perkins going to uphold the law when
the only result would be to risk getting
shot.

He frowned as he saw Rex leave the
others and head for the café. That
meant he was going to bother Clara
Long. She'd already complained about
him. Perkins hadn't done anything about
that either. Should he do anything now
or let Clara take her chances?

★ ★ ★

"Hello, Clara, darling," Rex called as he came in. "How's my favourite girl? You look as lovely as usual."

Clara didn't respond to this. "Would you like some coffee, Rex?"

"Yeah. OK." He pulled out a chair, sitting down, staring at her as she poured him the coffee.

Hoping her hand didn't shake she put the cup down on the table. As she did so his hand snaked out catching hold of her arm. She tried unsuccessfully to pull away.

"We've been away a long time. Did you miss me?"

"No."

"Course you did. I missed you. Still we should be home for a long while now, so we can see a lot of each other." When Clara said nothing, Rex frowned and decided to get nasty. "I hope you ain't got them Mexes still working for you."

"Who works for me is none of your business."

"I really wouldn't like it. And nor

would Pa. It ain't seemly for my girl to be involved with Mexes."

"I'm not your girl."

"I find 'em here I'm goin' to be almighty cross."

Clara managed to free herself at last. "Perhaps, Rex, you'd just better drink your coffee and leave."

"I like it when you get cross." Rex slurped his coffee noisily. "You gonna give me a kiss?"

"No. Are you going to pay for the coffee?"

"Only if you give me a kiss."

"In that case the coffee is on the house."

For a moment Rex didn't seem to know whether to be amused or angry. As usual he settled for sullen anger. "I dunno why you're so awkward, Clara. I don't see why you think yourself so much better than me."

"I'm not a thief or a cattle rustler. In my book that does make me better than you." Clara spoke as bravely as she could. But inside she was quaking and she had to clench her hands together so that Rex wouldn't see how much they shook.

As he glared at her, she wondered if perhaps she had gone too far in resisting him but before he could react, the door opened and Alf Perkins came in.

Clara didn't think much of Mr Perkins. She didn't think he even did his best. He was fat and lazy. He moaned a lot. But at that moment Clara was so pleased to see him she could have kissed *him*.

"Oh shit," Rex mumbled.

"Maybe you ought to join your father and brothers," Perkins advised. "There might not be any whiskey left iffen you don't."

"Yeah perhaps I'd better." Rex went to the door, then turned round and pointed a finger at Clara. "I'll see you later, darlin', and when I do you'd better be a bit more friendly."

As soon as he'd gone, Clara sank down on a chair, crossed her arms tightly across her chest and blinked back the tears that came into her eyes.

"Are you all right, Miss Clara?" Perkins asked.

"Thanks to you."

The man shrugged.

"Can't you do something about them? You're meant to be the law around here."

Perkins shrugged again and Clara knew she was being unfair to expect him to go up against the Forresters. It was a wonder he had come in to stop Rex from annoying her. If Rex complained to his father then, like Clara, Perkins too could find himself in trouble.

Conchita came nervously out of the kitchen and Clara put an arm round her. "What are we to do?"

"Keep out of their way," Perkins advised.

It angered Clara that they were helpless in the grip of the Forresters and she said, "It's not fair. Los

79

Santos would be such a nice place if it wasn't for them. As it is they've got everyone scared, waiting for their next appearance and wondering what they're going to do."

"It's just something we'll have to put up with until they decide to go away. They'll leave eventually, go on to pastures new, for one reason or another. In the meantime, don't worry too much, Miss Clara, they'll spend the rest of the time here in the saloon, getting drunk and they'll be gone come the morning."

"I hope so."

"But," Perkins added as a warning, "you might be wise to lock up and go home early. Both of you."

8

"C'MON, quick, let's go!" Lee leapt up into his saddle.

"You could stay here. They're not after you."

"Right now I ain't about to take that chance. Are you used to horses, Danny? Can you ride fast?"

Daniel grinned. "Be just like riding to hounds, old boy!" Mounting he took hold of his horse's reins and sent it in a gallop round the side of the adobe store, shouting, "Tally ho!"

Lee shook his head, feeling a bit bemused. Danny sure was a strange young man and he didn't know what he was talking about most of the time. But he was right when he said he could ride, he was already out of sight. And Lee was going to have to hustle to catch up with him and to lose the posse. The riders were almost on top of him.

There was no time to waste.

"Glad you decided to catch up, Pemberton." Daniel was picking a careful way through the rocks and scrub. "Which way, do you think?"

Lee paused to look round and consider. A distant line of cypress trees indicated the presence of a stream, with here and there outcrops of boulders. "That way. We can ride in the water then."

Immediately Daniel's bravado disappeared and he looked scared. "They won't have dogs with them, will they?"

"Doubt it. But the Marshal or one of the others might be good at tracking. If we're in the river they won't have any tracks to follow, will they?"

"Good idea, old boy."

★ ★ ★

"We've nearly got 'em!" Craig Weaver shouted. "They can't get away now!"

Marshal McCullum sighed. If it hadn't been for Craig and Johnny getting excited, yelling and firing their guns when it was obvious they had no hope of hitting anything, they might have been able to sneak up on Naughton and his unknown companion. As it was Naughton had been warned and the pair of them had taken off. And McCullum didn't share Craig's optimism. He'd seen too many prisoners escape from certain capture to become complacent.

They galloped past the trading store where Gibson watched, open mouthed, from the doorway.

Their quarry was already some way off, heading for the river.

★ ★ ★

As they neared the water, Daniel and Lee urged their horses on. Lee thought the posse was still too far away for anyone to hit them but he didn't want to take the chance. He wanted to get amongst the safety of the trees.

Once they came to the treeline, they bent low over their horses' backs, weaving a way towards the river. It wasn't far. With Daniel close behind, Lee rode down the rocky slope, across a bank of white pebbles and into the clear blue water.

"Which way?"

"West." Lee pointed. "It's the way we wanna go." He urged his horse along, but keeping it to a walk.

"Er, shouldn't we be going a bit faster?" Daniel's only thought was to get away as quickly as possible.

"We don't want to stir up the water too much. And keep to the middle of the stream where it's deepest. An expert tracker might still be able to tell the way we've gone but hopefully McCullum's tracker ain't an expert."

Daniel hoped Pemberton knew best. He decided not to argue the point. After all he wouldn't like it if a ranch foreman from Texas came to England and told him how to hunt a fox. He glanced back over his shoulder. So far there was no sight or sound of the men chasing them.

* * *

"Damn!" Craig swore. "They've gone in the river."

McCullum didn't need telling that. He could see for himself and it was what he too would have done. "Can you follow 'em?"

Craig eventually admitted. "I don't think I'm that good. But I reckon they'll have gone westwards."

"Makes sense. All right. Let's split up. Craig, you ride in the river see if you can spot anything. Johnny, take some of the men to the other bank, the rest of us'll ride along this side. They've got to come out somewhere."

* * *

After a while the river branched into two. While the main stream continued to meander on its westerly course, a second narrower stream wound down through the high rocky walls of a narrow canyon, where juniper trees clung to crevices.

"Let's go that way," Lee decided. "It'll be too easy to see us if we stick to the main channel. And be careful, it's a lot deeper."

As the water ran between the ever narrowing canyon walls, the current became much faster too. The streambed twisted and turned and jagged rocks appeared underfoot, making the going treacherous.

At one point Daniel's horse stuck its foot in a hole and Daniel fell off splashing into the stream.

"Are you all right?" Lee asked, riding back and reaching down to help him to his feet.

"Yes. Just wet." But Daniel found the water was running so fast it threatened to knock him over and he had to cling to his horse in order to stay upright.

"What about your horse?"

Daniel stroked its leg. "Seems all right to me. But I think we ought to get out of the river. It's getting dangerous."

"Yeah. I know. I've been looking for a spot."

And a few minutes later Lee found what he was searching for. Beyond a large group of rocks was a patch of sandy open ground leading to a brush covered slope which, although steep, he thought they could ride up without too much difficulty.

"The posse will see the horses' tracks," Daniel pointed out.

"Not if I brush them away."

"How?"

"With a branch of a tree. You ride over there and wait with the horses."

While he did so, Lee picked up a fallen branch and brushed it back and forth over the sand until he was satisfied that no tracks remained.

"I don't suppose it'll fool anyone for long but hopefully it'll fool the posse long enough so we can put some time between us."

* * *

Marshal McCullum pulled his horse to a halt. "Damn!" he said out loud. "Dammit all to hell! We've lost 'em."

"I was wrong," Craig admitted. "They must have taken that other stream we passed a while back."

"And I should have sent a couple of men that way to make sure. As it is they could be anywhere now! Damn!" McCullum looked up at the sky. They'd wasted several hours searching up and down the river and it was getting dark, the sun was low in the sky and already the valley was deep in shadow.

"We are going after 'em, ain't we?" Johnny asked anxiously.

"Yeah but not tonight. It'll be too dangerous. And come the morning I'll go on alone. Following 'em is my job and my problem, not any of your's. You've got businesses to run and homes to look after back in Juniper City."

Most of the men looked relieved.

It was one thing chasing round the countryside after fugitives but it was quite another when the chase might take days; or even weeks.

But neither Craig nor Johnny was pleased and Craig said, "You can't go up against 'em on your own."

"Oh, I don't think I have anything to fear from Mr Naughton."

"But you don't know who the other man is. He might be dangerous. And first you've got to pick up the trail again, which won't be easy."

"What are you suggesting?"

"I'm the best tracker you've got. You'll need my help. I'm going with you."

"What about the Rocking F ranch? Things have got to be sorted out there."

"Johnny can handle that, can't you?"

"Sure I can."

"Marshal, I want to be with you when you catch up with that bastard."

McCullum made up his mind quickly. "All right. I'll be glad of your company.

We'll set out in the morning as soon as it's light."

* * *

"Do you think the posse will give up?" Daniel asked hopefully as he and Lee began to ride across a wide meadow dotted with cottonwood trees, low bushes and prickly pear cactus.

"Would they in England?"

"We don't have posses in England."

"Well, would whatever law you do have give up if it was after a murderer?"

"No."

"Then Marshal McCullum won't give up either."

"I was afraid you'd say that."

9

"**M**IGUEL says Forrester and the others are in the saloon," Conchita said. "What you do, Clara?" She looked at her employer with anxious eyes, not just for Clara's sake but her own and Miguel's as well.

"I think we ought to do as Mr Perkins advised and lock up and go home." Clara didn't like giving into the gang and couldn't really afford the money she would lose by not serving dinner, but she could see no alternative. To stay open would be to risk her and Conchita getting hurt.

"Si, Clara, I think so too."

"And make sure Miguel stays indoors. If any of the Forresters see him and recognize him as working here . . . well, you know what'll happen."

"I will," Conchita promised. "He has studying to do."

"Off you go then. Hurry along. I'll see you in the morning." Clara wrapped a shawl round her shoulders, turned the sign hanging on the door to 'Closed' and carefully locked the door behind her. A few people were still around — talking, shopping — and some nodded to her. She acknowledged them absent-mindedly while making sure Rex Forrester wasn't laying in wait for her. As far as she was aware he didn't know where she lived and she didn't want him following her to find out.

She left the plaza behind, walking swiftly down the road by the side of the hotel and soon reached home. The two room adobe house was small, with a square yard out back, in which she was trying to grow vegetables.

She bolted shut the door firmly behind her, and went round making sure the windows were closed, pulling the shutters across them so that no one could see in. A prisoner in her own home, she thought angrily. Scared to go out, scared to stay in. Her only hope was that Mr Perkins would be right and the Forresters would stay in the saloon, drinking themselves into a stupor, and then leave in the morning. The trouble was they would always be back.

★ ★ ★

"I win, I believe, gentlemen." Bruce Forrester put down his cards, didn't even wait to see if anyone else had a better hand, and gathered in the pot of money. It wasn't often any of the town's citizens agreed to play with him or his sons — they usually disappeared as soon as they saw the family — but this time he'd bullied a few of the saloon's Mexican occupants into joining him. Cornered they knew better than to refuse or do anything other than let him win.

He smiled, revealing an almost toothless mouth, and indicated for the bartender to bring him over another beer; for which he naturally wouldn't pay.

His opponents glanced nervously at one another. Not only were they in danger of losing all their money but who knew whether or not Forrester and his sons might take it into their heads to beat them up? Or worse. In the minds of the gang Mexicans were put on earth merely to provide them with whatever pleasures they wanted to indulge in.

Forrester was wondering much the same thing, although as he was in a good mood, perhaps he'd let them be. It had been a profitable raid. Some cattle and horses and a lot of money. Enough that he could afford a few repairs round the ranch; Edith was always going on about the way she had to live so that would keep her quiet for a while. Maybe he'd even buy her a few fancy goods. She wasn't a bad wife after all. Did her best. He had stolen enough so that, except for raiding into Mexico, which didn't really count, they could stay at home for a while, take it easy. He was fifty-three and getting too old for all this riding round, risking getting shot. He should be taking it easier at his time of life.

And, most important, there was enough so that whenever they liked he and his sons could have a good time in town and they could all enjoy the whores.

Which Dirk had already done, for Forrester saw him come down the stairs buttoning up his trousers. And which Pat was in the process of doing by picking out which girl pleased him most.

And Rex, well Rex was all by himself at the end of the bar, moodily drinking whiskey because he was in love with Clara Long, and she, for some reason Forrester couldn't figure out, didn't want anything to do with him. She'd have to buck her ideas up and quick, because he didn't like one of his sons to be unhappy.

★ ★ ★

Miguel Delgado pressed his nose against the saloon's windows. He was meant to be in his bedroom studying but he wanted to make sure all the members of the Forrester gang were still inside and not about to bother Senorita Clara. So he had slipped out of his bedroom window and come down here. Conchita would kill him if she found out but he loved Senorita Clara and didn't want any harm to befall her.

Miguel was a quiet boy, badly affected by the death of his parents in an Apache raid a couple of years before. That had meant he and Conchita had had to leave the family's sheep farm in the foothills of the Mimbres Mountains and come to Los Santos, where a drunken, lazy uncle had taken them in. It was more a case of them looking after him than the other way round but at least he had provided them with a roof over their heads.

Then into their lives had come

Clara Long. If it hadn't been for her employing Conchita to help in the café, Miguel was sure his sister would have ended up as a whore in the saloon, entertaining the likes of Dirk and Pat and being ill treated by them too. And he himself would have followed his Uncle's example and become a drunk or maybe be destined to end up on the gallows. Instead, Senorita Clara was teaching him to read and write so he could follow a trade.

They both owed her a great deal and Miguel didn't like it when the Forresters were in town because he knew she was scared of them all and Rex especially. He wanted to protect her and wished he was older because, right now, all he could do was keep a watch out whereas what he really wanted to do was call Rex out and shoot him in a gunfight.

"Hey! Kid!" The voice disturbed his thoughts and he looked up to see that Dirk and Pat had emerged from the saloon. They must have seen him. "Come here, kid!"

Miguel wasn't going to do that. He span round taking off at a run. His heart pounded. How had they seen him? That didn't matter. They had. And the real question was what they would do to him if they caught him.

He was almost round the corner where alleys led between the Mexican hovels and he could make his escape amongst them, when a hand reached out and grabbed his arm. He was almost pulled off his feet as he was swung round to face the two out of breath young men.

"It is that damn kid works for Clara!" Dirk said triumphantly.

"Don't ask me. They all look alike to me."

"What you doin'? Spying on us? Eh?" Dirk shook the boy hard.

"No, senor, I wasn't, please," Miguel said, tears of fright spilling from his eyes. "Please, let me go. I mean no harm." He tried to wriggle free.

"Perhaps he knows where the Long bitch lives," Pat suggested. He too had seen how moody Rex was getting, especially when he'd learned that the café was already shut, and Rex in a mood was unpredictable and dangerous. "And perhaps," he thrust his face at Miguel, "he can be persuaded to tell us."

"Yeah." Dirk lifted Miguel off his feet and shook him again, making his teeth rattle.

"No, senor, no. I not know." But Miguel thought these men didn't believe him. That it didn't really matter to them whether he knew or not. They wanted to hurt him not only because he was a Mexican, but because he was also small and vulnerable. And he also knew that he wasn't. as brave as he was in his dreams when he faced up to and defeated these men. They would hurt him so bad he would betray Senorita Clara for the sake of himself. His only hope was escape . . .

Dirk slapped him round his face and

tugged at his hair, jerking his head back. "How many times I got to hit you, boy, before you tell me where Missy Long lives?"

"Please, senor."

Dirk hit him again and Miguel fell to the ground. He heard the men laugh and free for a moment seized his chance. Leaping to his feet, he dodged out of the way and ran to the corner, Dirk and Pat in loud pursuit. He had to get away. If they caught him again they'd kill him.

Sobbing with fright, Miguel ran into the nearest alleyway, which led between two houses, dashed across a courtyard, jumped over a wall and ran down another alley. He knew this section of town very well — he lived here — the Forresters didn't. Normally they never stopped in this part of Los Santos. Another yard, another alley and they were no longer behind him. Miguel collapsed in a doorway, hiding in the shadows, hugging his knees. He was crying as silently as he could — tears of shame, fear and anger.

"He's gone," Dirk said in disgust. "Little bastard. Hey you kid!" He raised his voice in a carrying yell. "Next time you won't get away so easily. You'd better believe that."

"Aw, c'mon, Dirk, he ain't worth it. Let's go."

"Guess you want a girl?"

"Yeah."

"OK." Dirk put an arm round his brother's shoulders. "And I could sure do with a drink. You're right. I don't feel much like beating up a Mexican kid not tonight and Rex's problems are his own. He'll have to learn how to handle 'em himself."

★ ★ ★

The following morning it looked as if Rex was going to attempt to do just that.

Bleary-eyed, hungover, father and three sons met in the livery stable where Forrester kicked the owner awake and ordered him to saddle their horses.

"And get a move on," he added, kicking him again. "Can't wait to see the old place and the old gal again."

"Pa." Rex spoke up hesitantly, not sure what sort of mood his father was in or how he would take what he was going to ask. Bruce liked the family to stay together, on the other hand he was a great one for romance. "Pa, you mind if I stay in town for a couple more days?"

"What for?" Forrester asked, while Dirk and Pat nudged one another.

While Rex blushed, Dirk said, "It's his love life he's worried about, Pa!"

"Oh yeah," Forrester grinned. "Ain't goin' too well is it, son?"

"Clara'll soon see reason," Rex said sulkily.

"I surely do hope so. All this moping around is gettin' on my nerves. OK, son, a couple of days. No more mind. I want you out at the ranch."

"OK, Pa," Rex agreed brightly. "That's all I'll need. And, Pa, can

I have some money?"

That didn't go down so well but grumpily Forrester let him have a few dollars.

"Good luck," Dirk said as he rode out, leaving Rex alone, and already plotting.

10

LOS SANTOS dozed in the afternoon sun.

So this had once been a Mexican town, Daniel, who had not been this far West before, thought. He couldn't say he was that impressed.

Most of the houses were tiny and looked as if they were falling down. A few had been repaired, patched up with pieces of tin or wood, others were left to decay. The streets were narrow and lined with rubbish. In one larger courtyard was a fountain, round which several plump dark skinned women had gathered to wash clothes and gossip at the same time. Men slept nearby protected from the sun by large sombreros and colourful serapes, while naked bimbos stood in whatever shade they could find, idly watching the two Americans riding through.

"Don't think much of it huh?" Lee asked, with a grin.

"Definitely not." But then Daniel spotted two dark eyed, black haired senoritas standing in a doorway. They wore white off-the-shoulder blouses and skirts showing their ankles. Ankles, hmmm! Perhaps it wasn't so bad after all.

The road led to the main plaza in the middle of which was another fountain. Not that there was much even here — a few stores, a café, a small hotel and a couple of saloons. Porches along the fronts of the buildings offered welcome shade. The sidewalks were cracked and splintered in places and the road was nothing more than dust.

Across another road was the court-house, signs telling visitors it also housed the Town Constable's office — keep well away from that, Daniel thought — a lawyer's and the real estate office. While built of adobe like everything else, it was two storeys high and the windows had ornate iron grilles around them.

"It was probably once the residence of the Mexican governor," Lee said as they rode by to look for the livery stable.

"What are we going to do now we're here?"

"Take our time."

"What about McCullum?"

"We've left him far behind. We ain't got the need to rush into anything. We'll find out what we can about the Forresters and where they might be before we go after 'em. Let's stable our horses, then go and have something to eat in that café we passed. I don't know about you but I'm hungry. And someone there will be able to tell us where we can get a cheap room."

★ ★ ★

"Home, sweet home," Bruce Forrester said as he clumped his way into the ranchhouse. "Edith! We're here! Where's our dinner?"

His wife hurried out from the kitchen, wiping her hands on her apron. "It'll be ready in a minute."

"Why ain't it ready now?"

Edith didn't bother to ask how she could be expected to have their meal ready when she didn't know they were coming home. She had long known better than to argue.

"Everything all right here?"

"Yes."

"Good." Forrester was satisfied. The small ranch hidden in the hills was a good hide-out from any law on both sides of the border. Stolen cattle, stolen goods, other outlaws on the run were all safe here.

"Where's Rex?" Edith suddenly asked anxiously as she didn't see her youngest son. "Is he all right?"

The men all looked at one another and laughed. Forrester said, "He's stayed in town. He's got a date with Miss Clara Long."

Edith put a hand to her mouth. Rex might be her youngest, her baby, that didn't stop her realizing what he was capable of when he didn't get his own way. Although Edith didn't know Clara very well, she so seldom went to Los Santos she hardly knew anyone there, from what she had seen Clara appeared to be a nice young woman. She didn't deserve to be hurt.

"What's the master?" Forrester asked harshly.

"N . . . nothing."

"Get our dinner then. We're hungry. Let's go wash up, boys."

The three men dropped their coats and saddlebags on the floor, leaving Edith to run round after them, clearing up.

Yeah, Forrester decided, she was a good wife, uncomplaining, easy to bully, but she did worry so; about them, their way of life and the dangers. And that was something he'd never been able to cure her of, however much he tried.

★ ★ ★

"What would you like to eat?" Clara asked the two tired looking strangers who had taken a seat by the window.

"Beefstew and coffee," Lee said.

"Me too," Daniel added, beefstew and coffee being about the only items on the menu that didn't have Mexican sounding names.

"Be right with you."

"No one here looks very happy, do they?" Daniel said, glancing round at the café's few other customers. In most places he'd been the citizens were willing to talk to strangers, too willing most of the time. Here no one seemed to want to take any notice of them, averting their eyes, keeping their heads down. Not that he was complaining. He was used to English inhibitions amongst strangers but it was unusual to say the least.

"I guess it's got something to do with the Forrester gang. We'd better be careful, Danny, we don't know if they've got any friends, or spies, here in town. We don't want them learning we're after 'em."

When Clara came back with their food, Daniel said, "Can we see the owner?"

"The owner?"

"Yes. You know, the man who employs you."

"Why? Is anything wrong?"

"No. We just want to ask him a question."

"You can speak to me."

"I told you," Daniel's voice rose grumpily — was she stupid or deaf? "We want to see the owner."

"I am the owner."

Daniel gaped at her. "You? But you're a girl!"

"I'm glad you realized."

"Don't take any notice of him," Lee said, an amused glint in his eyes. "He's from England. I guess women in England don't own cafés."

"They most certainly don't! English women know their place!"

"Luckily out here women have minds of their own!" Clara banged Daniel's stew down so hard some of it spilt over the top of the plate.

"Now look what you've done."

"I'm so sorry, sir, I'll get a cloth and wipe it up. I expect you consider that's my sort of work."

As she stalked away, Daniel leant across to Lee. "You know, Pemberton, I can't stand or indeed understand that sort of woman. Why do they want to be independent? Why can't they be content obeying men who obviously know best?"

Clara, who had heard this last remark, practically flung the cloth at Daniel and said icily, "Was there anything else?"

"Yes, ma'am," Lee said as politely as he could, hoping that the girl didn't think he felt the same as his partner. "We need a room for a couple of nights but we ain't got much money. Is the hotel dear?"

"No. Even you should be able to afford it! Now, if there's nothing more, I've got more important work to do than to stand around talking to you."

"You've annoyed her."

"Typical, old boy. Most women can't take reasonable criticism or advice."

"I don't see how you can give anyone advice."

"What do you mean?"

"Well the messes you get yourself into you obviously don't know what's best for yourself let alone anyone else!"

Daniel sat back, a sulky look on his face. The annoying thing about Lee was that he was almost always right. But Daniel couldn't admit that. "The messes I get into are mostly the fault of other people." The other annoying thing about Lee was the way he grinned at him as if he wasn't fooled by Daniel and didn't think Daniel was either.

★ ★ ★

Daniel surveyed the room he and Lee were to share in some dismay. It could be worse, he supposed; at least there were two beds so they wouldn't have to share a bed as well. But they didn't look in the least bit comfortable — being narrow, with lumpy mattresses, thin pillows and a motheaten blanket each. No sheets naturally. Neither were there any cupboards, only hooks for their clothes. One rug on the floor, a narrow window, and one towel — the washbasin being in a room along the corridor and shared by all the guests on this floor.

If he was ever going to get any sleep, which was doubtful, Daniel knew he'd have to be very drunk.

"I'm going over to the saloon," he announced as Lee stretched out on one of the beds. "You coming?"

"Don't think I will. I'm bushed. I want to think about what we're going to do. I also don't want any of the gang to see me in case they recognize me."

"Do you think they're in town?" Daniel wondered whether he should stay in as well after all.

"No. But I don't wanna take the chance. And Danny."

"Yes?" Daniel paused with his hand on the door knob.

"Be careful."

"So you keep telling me. Don't worry. I know you believe I'm irresponsible but I'm not completely stupid."

"All right," Lee grinned at him. "Don't gamble all your remittance money away."

Why did Pemberton always have to have the last word? Daniel thought crossly. For he couldn't say anything in return to that because there had been many times in the past when he had in fact been completely stupid enough to lose everything on the turn of a card!

11

LOS SANTOS at night wasn't much more exciting than during the day. Nor much friendlier. But Daniel was pleased to find the two saloons doing good business. He went into the larger of the two and stared round in satisfaction. He had money in his pocket and here he'd be sure to find something to spend it on: a drink, a poker game, maybe even a girl. And if he was lucky he might pick up some gossip about the Forrester gang.

★ ★ ★

Still angry over the Englishman's comments about her and about independent women, Clare locked up and saying goodnight to Conchita started to walk home. As soon as she turned the corner by the hotel she was alone. Most people were already indoors and those who weren't were congregating by the saloons. She was tired. It had been a long day, busy too. She also wanted to get home, relax . . .

"Hi, Clara." The man stepped out of the shadows and stood in front of her, barring her way.

It was Rex Forrester.

Heart beating fast with fright and shock, Clara came to a halt. "Oh! You startled me! I thought you'd left town."

"I suppose you'll say you'd have liked that. But I stayed behind. To see you."

Clara couldn't resist glancing round.

Rex laughed. "The Constable ain't here tonight."

Nor was anyone else. Clara could hear shouts coming from the saloons, the sound of a honkytonk piano. It made her feel even more isolated. And afraid. "I don't know what you mean, Rex. Now please let me go by. I'm tired and I want to go home."

"You ain't goin' anywhere without me." And he took hold of her arm in a painfully firm grip.

"Let me go," Clara said, dismayed at the panic in her voice.

"You an' me are goin' together."

"No!"

"Yeah. You know you want me as much as I want you. Be a good girl. Show me a good time."

"Over my dead body."

"It ain't your body that'll be dead," Rex said ominously. "You make any fuss and I'll kill that little Mexican whore works for you. Ain't but what she deserves anyhow."

"My, my what a lovely way to woo a girl," Clara said sarcastically.

"Shut up and come on."

As Rex started to pull her along the street, Clara struggled and cried out once, long and loud before Rex clamped a hand over her mouth, cutting off her scream.

"Ain't no call for that, darlin'. It

won't do you any good."

Clara found herself dragged forward. She felt cold with fear. Even if anyone had heard her, it was doubtful they would come to her rescue, especially when they saw she was in the clutches of Rex Forrester.

* * *

The scream disturbed Lee, who was just dozing into sleep. Wondering if he had imagined it, but not really believing so, he got off the bed and went over to the window. Away from the plaza, Los Santos didn't have any street lights but the moon was bright enough for him to see the man and woman in the road below. They were struggling, the woman clearly not wanting to go where the man was taking her.

And suddenly Lee recognized the nice girl from the café. Clara her name was.

Los Santos might be the sort of place where girls often screamed — but not nice ones. Without stopping to think, he grabbed up his gun, sticking it in his belt, shrugging on his coat as he went. He left the hotel, running down its side, to where the couple were just crossing the far street.

"Let her be!" he yelled.

The couple stopped, turning in his direction and with a pounding heart Lee recognized the man as one of those who had robbed and killed Mr Rice. He was tempted to pull his gun and shoot him. But he couldn't do that with the girl there to see him do it. And at the moment she was his main concern.

"Keep out of it," Rex warned. "It ain't nothin' to do with you."

Lee came to a halt near them. "It is when you're obviously forcing your attentions on someone. Are you all right, Miss Clara?"

"Clara! How the hell do you know my girl! How dare you call her Clara!"

"Oh don't be so silly," Clara said crossly.

119

"Where the hell does he know you from?"

"He and his friend came into my café earlier today. He doesn't know my surname so naturally he's got to call me Clara. And, Rex, I am not your girl."

"Why don't you let her go?" Lee repeated. "And we can forget all about this."

"Shut up," Rex snarled. "You interfere with my girl, I'm goin' to teach you a lesson you ain't likely to forget." And letting go of Clara he dashed towards Lee, fists raised.

Lee sidestepped the young man's rush and the swing of his arm and brought his own fist up. It caught Rex in the chest and he stumbled backwards, gasping for breath.

"You bastard!" he yelled and came at Lee again, only for Lee to hit him hard round the jaw. Rex fell on his back the fight gone from his eyes.

"Get up! And then get outa here!"

Lee pulled Rex to his feet and shoved him away. "Go on, go!"

Rex pointed a shakey finger at him. "You just watch out, that's all! You'll have me and my Pa to answer to!"

"Do tell."

Glaring at him, Rex walked off, anger and humiliation in every line of his body.

As he went, Clara sagged against the wall. Lee caught hold of her. "Are you OK?"

"I am now. He was going . . . going to . . . "

"I know exactly what the bastard was going to do," Lee said grimly. Clara suddenly burst into tears and he held her close to his chest, murmuring, "You're all right. You're safe. He's gone."

Clara sniffed, wiping her nose. "You don't understand. That was Rex Forrester. He's not only got a Pa, he's got three brothers as well. None of them will let an insult go by."

Lee stared in the direction Rex had gone. "Well, if he wants a fight with me, I certainly want one with him."

"What do you mean?"

"It's a long story. Can I see you home?"

"I live just round the corner. I can manage on my own."

"Hey, I don't mean you any harm."

"I know that." She smiled at him. "I just don't want to put you to any more bother."

"It's no bother."

"Then I would like your company," Clara admitted. "Where's your friend? The snooty Englishman."

"He's gone gambling. Look, Miss . . . ?"

"Long. But Clara will do fine."

"Lee Pemberton. Look, Clara, Danny and me are both after the Forresters, for different reasons, and I think you can tell us something about them. Will you?"

"Is this all part of your long story?"

"Yeah."

"In that case perhaps you'd like to

fetch your friend while I make us some coffee."

"Would you mind?"

Clara shook her head. "I was sleepy before but I'm wide awake now."

"I'll be as quick as I can."

★ ★ ★

Daniel looked up in surprise as he saw Lee hurrying across the room towards him. "What's wrong?"

"Nothing, not really. Can you come with me? Lee bent forward and added quietly so only Daniel could hear, "I've found someone willing to tell us about the Forresters."

Daniel looked at the money in front of him and the cards in his hands. Things hadn't exactly been going well. It might be just as well to quit now before he lost any more. "Let me finish this hand, then I'll be with you."

As they left the saloon, he said, "Who are we going to see?"

"Miss Clara Long."

"Who?"

"The girl from the café."

"Oh! Her!"

"Be kind to her, Danny. She was almost raped tonight by Rex Forrester."

"What! Bloody hell! How do you know?"

"I rescued her."

Daniel stared at his companion in amazement. Honestly, leave some people alone for five minutes and they got into all sorts of scrapes! And Lee had the cheek to criticize him!

"She lives just down here."

* * *

Rex decided to leave Los Santos. He was brave enough in the company of his father and brothers, or when bullying a young woman. On his own he was a coward. He didn't want to risk meeting the cowboy again.

He saddled and bridled his horse, not being gentle about it. How dare that bastard, whoever he was, interfere! How dare he call Clara, Clara! Rex hadn't handled the situation very well. He should have shot the bastard. Made Clara see that if she made up to other men she'd get them hurt. Made her see he was the only one for her. But it was too late. And now all Rex wanted to do was get away before anyone else found out how he'd been bested by a girl and a damn cowboy.

What would he tell his brothers and his father when he arrived home early? He couldn't tell them the truth. Dirk and Pat would laugh at him and his father would hit him for being a coward. Yet he couldn't say he'd had his way with Clara. They'd be sure to find out he'd lied and that would make the situation worse.

No, the best thing would be to say that several men had come to her rescue: too many for even a Forrester to handle on his own. They'd threatened him, pulled their guns on him, driven him out of town.

Yeah, that sounded all right.

And then his father would help him get revenge on that damn cowboy and on Clara too. And that sounded all right as well.

12

CLARA put a coffeepot and a plate of home-made biscuits down on the table. "Help yourselves, please."

Daniel stared round the room. It was L-shaped, with the kitchen situated in the smaller section, and plain with white walls, and little furniture — just the table, four chairs and a couple of comfortable chairs either side of the window. But Clara had made an effort to brighten it up, with colourful curtains matching the tablecloth and a vase of flowers on a shelf, and it was very clean and tidy. A rug lay in the middle of the floor. Candles lit up the area round where they sat.

As Clara joined them, Lee said, "Clara, this is Danny by the way."

"Daniel actually. Daniel Phipps-Naughton," Daniel said, without much hope of being taken notice of.

He and Clara looked at one another warily, not knowing what to make of each other. Not liking each other much either.

"You weren't hurt, were you?"

Clara shook her head. "No. But I'm scared that Rex is never going to take no for an answer." She smiled weakly. "But that's my problem and I'll have to sort it out. Now, Lee, you said both you and Danny . . . "

Daniel sighed heavily.

" . . . were after the Forresters."

"That's right." And Lee quickly told the girl what had happened, how they'd met — Daniel wasn't too happy about her knowing he'd been in jail, nor that he was a remittance man, although she didn't seem to take much notice of either — and why they'd joined up.

She frowned. "Well, don't expect help from anyone here."

"What I can't understand is why the law doesn't do something about the Forresters," Daniel said. "I mean they seem to ride around doing whatever they want. Everyone knows who they are and where they live, yet no one comes after them. It wouldn't happen in England. They'd have been hung on the gallows by now."

"I think some of it is to do with the fact that there's so much open space out here," Lee said. "How long did it take us to get here from Juniper City?"

"Three days. A very long three days," Daniel complained. "Riding all day, sleeping out in the open on the hard ground, which I must say isn't a bit like camping out in England where I would have had a tent, a campbed and a servant . . . "

"Well I did most of the work and all the cooking for you."

"Yes and burnt offerings it was too."

Lee ignored this criticism. "And Juniper City only had a town marshal. The nearest sheriff is even further away. And he's responsible for a large area and catching a great many outlaws.

He's in one place the Forresters are in another."

"And they can always escape over the border into Mexico," Clara added. "The law can't follow them there unless the Mexicans agree to it which they don't very often. And from what I've heard their place in the hills is a fortress. It would take a large posse to go out there, not just a sheriff and his deputy."

"And they'd have plenty of warning to get away."

"Exactly."

"Do you mind telling us all you know about the gang? This is good coffee by the way."

"Thank you."

Lee and Clara looked at one another and smiled.

"Well, I suppose if the two of you are foolish enough to even consider going out to the Forresters' hide-out, then the least I can do is help you all I can. Are you sure you want to go?"

Daniel had long since decided he

certainly didn't want to but Lee was saying, "We must."

"I'm not sure exactly where their place is. I don't think anyone here in town does know, except perhaps for some of the Mexicans and they're too scared of the Forresters to say so. It was once owned by a Mexican grandee who left it to fall into ruin after the War with Mexico. No one moved in to take his place because there are still times when any lonely ranch is likely to be subject to attacks by bands of Apaches."

Indians, Daniel thought grumpily, that was all he needed.

"The mountains are isolated, remote. The only people who live there are a few sheepherders, mostly Mexicans, who have always braved the Apaches, or other foreigners. And they keep very much to themselves."

"When did the Forresters come here?"

"Oh, quite a while ago now. Summer last year." Clara shivered at the memory. "Los Santos was a quiet place. Everyone — Americans and Mexicans got along and while it was never going to be a prosperous town, it was doing all right. There was talk about making improvements, putting in more lighting, building a school, that sort of thing. Since the gang came things have been getting steadily worse."

"We noticed no one said much to us," Daniel said. "People looked frightened."

"They're not like that all the time. But the Forresters had just been in town. They'd caused trouble as usual. There was a fight over one of the girls at the saloon, someone was beaten up. They didn't pay for anything. But worst of all they have this down on Mexicans. No one was badly hurt this time but last time they were here a Mexican was shot and killed."

"And no one does anything about it?"

"No, Danny, they don't dare."

"Haven't you got any law?"

"Alf Perkins, the Town Constable. He's not going to go up against the Forresters when his job is to collect taxes, catch stray dogs and take bribes from the saloon-keepers."

Lee said, "But with only four of 'em in the gang surely there are enough men here in town who could get together and go up against 'em."

"Ah but you see their ranch is used by other outlaws on their way to and from Mexico, or those who just want a good place to hide out in for a while. While they're there they take part in rustling raids, look after the cattle and do other odd jobs round the place. That's another reason why no one wanted to speak to you. They thought you were on the run and headed for the hills."

"Did we look as if we were?" Daniel asked disbelievingly.

"Yes," Clara bluntly replied.

"And the outlaws would join the Forresters in fighting any challenge from the town?"

"Yes, or so people here believe."

"And . . . er . . . are any other outlaws there at this precise time?"

"Bound to be."

"Oh dear."

Lee didn't look a great deal happier than Daniel did. Going up against four men was one thing. Going up against four men who had help from an unspecified number of other outlaws was something else entirely.

"Also out there is Edith, Forrester's wife. She's a poor down-trodden timid woman, who whenever I've seen her is drooping with fatigue. Goodness knows what sort of life she leads but it must be dreadful." And unfortunately it was what Rex wanted for her. "Now, gentlemen, can I get you any more coffee?"

"No, thanks," Lee said. "We'll have to be going soon. Are you sure you'll be all right here on your own?"

"Oh yes. Rex doesn't know where I live and I expect after what happened he's ridden out of town with his tail well between his legs. The look on his face!" And Clara laughed.

"How long have you lived here?" Lee asked her.

"In Los Santos? Ten years now. I used to live in Santa Fe but when my mother died, Pa moved here."

"So the café is his really?" Daniel asked hopefully.

Clara laughed. "No, Mr Naughton, the café is all mine. A couple of years ago Pa decided to go to California. Start anew again. I didn't want to do that. So I stayed behind."

"On your own? And he let you?"

"Of course he let me. Anyway he didn't have any say in the matter."

"In England a girl has to do as her father tells her." Daniel couldn't imagine any of his sisters not doing what they were told. Or imagine his father not handing out his orders, expecting them to be obeyed.

"It's a good job I'm not English then. Why should I have to leave everything behind and go somewhere strange just because my father wants me to? Oh, I know, it's because he's a man and I'm a mere woman who cannot possibly know what's best and who needs looking after. As a dutiful son did you always do what you were meant to?"

"Of course I didn't. I wouldn't be here now if I had."

"I suppose you'll say it's different for a man."

"It is."

"How?"

"It just is."

"Oh really!" Clara exclaimed and turning back to Lee, who was much more sensible, said, "How on earth can you stop yourself hitting him?" before changing the subject from herself back to the Forresters. "What do the two of you intend to do when you find them?"

Daniel and Lee looked at one another and Lee admitted, "We ain't really thought about that. I suppose my idea was to ride in, shooting, kill a couple of 'em, haul the others off to the Marshal and get them to confess to what they'd done. That doesn't seem likely now."

"No. You can't handle them on your own."

"Perhaps the best thing to do is scout round, find out where their hide-out is, then contact the law and lead a sheriff there. I don't know. We'll think of something, won't we Danny?"

"We'll have to, or you won't get your boss's money back and I won't clear my name." But Daniel no longer believed they'd do either. Much more likely was that they'd get shot.

"I wish there was more I could do to help."

"You've done more than enough. At least now we're warned of what we're up against." Lee stood up. "See you in the morning, Clara."

"Yes. Goodnight, Lee, Danny."

As they walked back through the dark towards the hotel, Lee said, "I'm sorry if I've got you into something dangerous."

"Yes, well, I suppose some of it was also my fault," Daniel graciously admitted.

"What do you think of Clara now you know her better?"

"She's still too independent for me." Daniel glanced slyly at Lee. "But you like her don't you, Pemberton, old boy?" And he was sure that even in the darkness he saw the man redden.

13

LEE went red again the following morning, and so did Clara, when they saw one another in the café. Clara brought over his and Daniel's breakfasts and said, "Are you still going?"

"Yeah. As soon as we've eaten and made sure we've got all we need."

"I wish you weren't."

So do I, Daniel thought. The night before he'd tried to get Lee to change his mind, to see their quest as impossible. Lee had proved obstinate. He'd threatened that if Daniel wouldn't go with him he'd go on his own, and he hadn't taken any notice when Daniel threatened in turn to let him do just that. Why, Daniel wondered, was Lee right and why was he here, getting ready to set out into danger? Talk about Daniel in the lion's den!

"We'll be careful," Lee promised. Once the girl had gone to serve her other customers he turned to Daniel. "Have you got spare ammunition?"

"Yes."

"I don't think we need much really. Just a few supplies in case we have to stay out overnight, that's about all. We might as well start once we've finished here."

"All right," Daniel agreed and wondered if he was eating the equivalent of the condemned prisoner's last meal.

★ ★ ★

It had taken Marshal McCullum and Craig Weaver a long time to find Daniel's trail again. By the time they did the pair they were chasing had almost a day's start on them. But either believing that the trail wouldn't be found or that the posse would give up — or maybe just being in a hurry to get to wherever they were going — they had made no further attempt to hide their tracks' making them easy to follow.

"It looks like they're heading for Mexico," Craig said.

"Yeah, wouldn't you? Even an Englishman will believe he's safe there because I can't follow him across the border."

"I can."

McCullum's eyes narrowed. "None of that sort of talk, young man. You'd be breaking the law as much as Naughton."

"I wouldn't be murdering anyone!"

"Even so I couldn't let you do it."

"So you'd let the bastard get away with what he's done?" Craig was mutinous. "Doesn't sound right to me."

"No, I won't let him get away with it! I reckon he'll have to come back some time to collect his remittance . . ."

"We'll have gone back to Juniper City by then, unless you're suggesting we wait on the border for him."

"No," McCullum shook his head. "That would be a waste of time. He could cross back anywhere Texas, Arizona, even California. What I will do is send out telegraphs and Wanted posters asking other lawmen to keep an eye open in case he ends up in their territory. I can send the same information to the railroads and stage companies in case he tries to head East or to Northern California."

"Do you think he will?"

"He might. He might even try to get home to England. But whatever he decides to do he'll need money for it, so I'll notify the banks as well so they can watch out for him either collecting his remittance or telling 'em where he wants it sent. Who knows? The authorities in Mexico might even be willing to help us. Don't worry, Craig, I want the little sonofabitch caught as much as you do. He'll be arrested sooner or later."

"OK, Marshal," Craig said, still wondering if it would be possible to cross the border without McCullum stopping him. Having Naughton arrested at some time in the future was all very well but it wasn't nearly so satisfying as the thought of taking revenge personally.

"There's a town a few miles up ahead. Los Santos. It ain't much of a place but Naughton might have gone there to rest up and buy supplies. We'll make enquiries see if anyone has spotted him. Maybe he'll even still be there." Although McCullum didn't sound very hopeful about that.

"And if he ain't?"

"Then we might as well turn back."

"Not go all the way to the border?"

"Can't see the point. And the sooner I get those flyers out the better."

★ ★ ★

Lee pulled the girth on the saddle tight and did it up, patting his horse at the same time. He checked his gun and making sure the hammer was down on an empty chamber, slid it back into the holster. "Ready?"

"Yes." Daniel had finished saddling his animal.

"Don't look so worried, Danny, there won't be any danger, not iffen we're careful."

Famous last words, Daniel thought. Why was this happening to him? Why wasn't he home, safe and well in England? Why on earth was he of all people riding out into the foothills in search of a gang of cutthroat outlaws? Perhaps, he hoped forlornly, they wouldn't find the hide-out, although he had the uncomfortable feeling that Lee Pemberton would continue to look until he was successful.

And what would they do if they did find it?

What would he do if they didn't? He'd still be wanted for murder.

Oh, what a tangled mess!

As they rode out of town, Clara and the little Mexican girl who worked for her, both came out of the café to wave them goodbye. Were they ever going to see them again?

★ ★ ★

"Here you are, dear." Edith put the mug of coffee down on the rickety porch where Forrester sat in the chair, leaning back, surveying the corrals. He didn't thank her — he never did — and she hurried away before he could find fault with the drink and shout at her.

Forrester hardly noticed. Idly he picked up the mug, sipping at the coffee. He hardly tasted it either. He was busy thinking, which was something that didn't come easily to him.

He didn't believe Rex's story that ten men had come between him and Clara and that he'd had to fight his way out of town. The townsmen would never dare go up against any of the Forresters for fear of retaliation. And if this stranger — a cowboy who was friendly with Clara — had had nine

145

friends with him then Rex would never have suffered just one bruise on his face. Rex must have been reading those dime novels again to come up with a story like that.

But he did believe that Rex had been humiliated and he didn't like that. He didn't like to see any of his sons hurt, and Rex was his favourite.

He wondered who the cowboy was. Whoever he was he needed teaching a lesson.

And so did Miss Clara Long. This was all her fault. It was time she was shown she had no reason to be so arrogant, thinking herself better than Rex. She, along with everyone else, was about to find out they had to bow to the Forresters' will. He didn't really believe the citizens of Los Santos had guts enough to make a stand but you just never knew and it wouldn't do any harm to remind them of the fact that they were cowards. As soon as he could rouse himself they'd ride back into town.

* * *

"Do you think those two newcomers were on their way to join the Forresters?" Doctor Round asked.

"Dunno." Alf Perkins and the Doctor were playing crib for a penny a game and enjoying several glasses of whiskey at the same time. "But I saw 'em leaving town a short while ago so I expect they were. They looked the type. One was English and you know what they're like."

Round picked up and shuffled the cards. "I'm scared they'll do something really bad soon. They're getting wilder all the time, especially Bruce and Dirk. Dirk hurt one of the saloon girls this time. He beat her up while Pat watched. Badly. Couldn't you contact the law up in Sante Fe about them?"

"I'll think about it."

"Well don't think too long or it might be too late." Doctor Round stood up, taking the bottle of whiskey with him, and went over to the window. Two men were dismounting outside. "Oh, oh you've got company, Alf."

"Oh, who?"

"Don't recognize 'em but they look like lawmen to me."

★ ★ ★

"It's hot." Daniel paused to pull his bandanna from his neck, take off his hat and wipe his forehead.

Lee drank from his canteen, handing it to Daniel. The water was warm.

They'd been riding for about three hours and the sun was high in a blue, cloudless sky. There was no breeze and the little grass there was, was already turning brown.

Daniel hoped they weren't lost. The hills, high and foreboding, crowded in on all sides, buttes reaching up into the sky; the colours red, orange and rusty brown. The only vegetation was stunted juniper trees and mesquite bushes clinging to the sides of the hills. Dust rose up from their horses' hooves.

"And people actually fight over this land?" Daniel said, thinking of the Apache raids and hoping there weren't any Indians hiding in the rocks right now.

"Sometimes. Don't you think it has a sort of wild beauty?"

"No, I bloody don't! It's not a bit like the green fields of Kent. Why sometimes there we even have rain! Pemberton, do you know where we're going? Or where we've been?"

"Of course I do. We go this way." While Lee sounded confident and as determined as ever, he hadn't expected to find the land so empty and desolate, despite what Clara had said. They could ride round for days amongst the shadowed canyons and valleys and never catch a glimpse of the Forresters' hide-out. But he wasn't going to admit that to Daniel, not just yet.

★ ★ ★

149

Rex Forrester stood by the corral watching one of the outlaws hiding out at the ranch breaking a wild horse. He wasn't having much success and had been bucked off several times so far. On the far side of the wall, Dirk and Pat were talking and laughing with a couple of the others but Rex had the feeling they were laughing at him, rather than at the horsebreaker. That they didn't believe his story.

It wasn't fair. Even his mother hadn't been very sympathetic. Rex was determined to show them he wasn't a coward, or a loser in love, and in order to do that he would have to make sure Clara and her cowboy friend were both sorry. How, he wasn't yet sure.

"Hey, someone's coining!" Dirk suddenly called, and pointed to a rider approaching at a gallop.

Rex recognized Little Joey, one of the men who'd been here some time, and who preferred the company of cattle to the family who were hiding him.

The three brothers broke away from

the corral and hurried up to the house, where Little Joey was headed. What was wrong now?

They arrived there almost at the same time as Little Joey pulled his horse to a halt in front of their father, who had climbed to his feet.

"What's the matter?" Forrester asked harshly.

"We've got company."

14

"WHAT'S that up there?" Daniel asked.

"Where?"

"A glinting amongst the rocks. See?" Daniel pointed.

Lee followed his gaze. "Oh shit!"

"What . . . ?"

Something whined by Daniel's ear followed an instant later by the crack of a rifleshot. Before he could do or say anything, another bullet smashed into the ground right by his horse's front hooves. Startled, the animal reared and, taken by surprise, Daniel tumbled back out of the saddle.

Lee was already pulling his rifle from its scabbard and at the same time he made a grab for Daniel's horse. He missed and the animal took off at a gallop, back down the way they'd come. "Danny! You OK?"

A bit dazed but otherwise unhurt Daniel struggled to his feet. More shots hit the ground round them and he moaned, "Oh, God." They were going to die.

Lee held out a hand intending to pull Daniel up behind him, but his horse was jittery, sidling this way and that and all the time bullets were still singing in the air round them. It was too dangerous to stay in the open any longer.

"Make for the rocks!" he shouted. Amongst their safety they could decide whether to stay and fight or run.

Daniel took off at a dash for the shelter of some large boulders, while Lee paused to fire back at their ambushers, before starting to follow him. Daniel was halfway there when a bullet struck Lee in the ribs. He gasped, dropped the rifle, and fell sideways just about managing to stay in the saddle.

"Pemberton!" Daniel came to a halt, not knowing what to do. "Lee!"

He ought to go to Lee, help him, but his feet seemed stuck to the ground and he couldn't move. Another bullet went precariously close to the wounded man. What should he do? Then with Lee somehow clinging to the saddle, the horse galloped away. Daniel's problem was solved. Now all he had to do was save himself.

Followed by more bullets, he raced for the rocks, leaping amongst them and collapsed to the ground, breathing heavily. Somehow the Forresters had discovered their presence in the hills and were shooting at them. What would they do? Let them go or come after them? Daniel almost sobbed with fear.

He drew his gun but his hand was shaking so much he shoved it back in the holster, scared he'd only shoot himself. He had to find somewhere to hide in case the gang did come to look for him.

★ ★ ★

Lee urged his horse on down the valley. He held the wound with one hand, trying to stop it bleeding, but already his shirt was soaked down one side. After the first numbness it hurt like hell and blackness kept threatening him but he had to hang on, get away as far as he could, or the ambushers would find him and complete the job.

★ ★ ★

"You've got one of 'em!" Pat cried, banging Dirk on the back. "Good shot!"

"But he got away," Forrester pointed out. "And the other one has gone too. Come on let's get down there. Finish the bastards off."

"You think they're lawmen?" Rex asked his father.

"Nope. Sheriffs are stupid but not that stupid they'd come after us without a large posse to back 'em up. But it don't really matter who they are, does it? No one comes near me and mine and gets away with it."

* * *

Daniel slid and slithered through the rocks, not caring that he was tearing his clothes or cutting his hands on sharp stones. He made his way deeper and deeper into their shelter. Suddenly he heard voices. It was them!

"Oh, God, no," he whispered to himself. Where could he hide? Up ahead were two rocks, one balanced precariously on top of the other. If he could push himself in between them he surely wouldn't be seen. Breathing raggedly he moved in their direction.

* * *

Lee glanced back. His heart twisted in panic as he saw two riders enter the valley and gallop in his direction. Hurt as he was he couldn't outride them. He urged his horse up the side of the hill, twisting and turning through the rocks and trees, hoping to find a place to hide or make one last stand.

* * *

"There's one of the bastards!" Rex shouted. "Let's get him!"

* * *

Lee reached the top of the ridge. As he did so he slid off the horse, which immediately came to a halt nearby. Lee sat down, exhausted. He should mount up again, but he lacked the energy or the will. As it was it took all the effort he could muster to stand up. The men were somewhere below him. He weaved to the edge and peered over to the valley floor a long way below. He was in danger of tumbling forward and down. Then his blurred eyes spotted what looked like the entrance to a cave.

Blinking away tears of pain, wishing everything wouldn't keep swaying blackly around him, Lee inched his way down the sandy slope, clinging to rocks and bushes, fearing he was going to fall.

He came to the dark opening he'd seen. It wasn't really a cave, just a slash in the hillside. But it was his only hope of escape. He slid into it and somehow managed to grab hold of some branches of a bush growing nearby, pulling them in front of the opening. He didn't know if it hid the cave from his pursuers. He no longer cared very much. All he wanted to do was close his eyes and give into the darkness which would take away the pain.

He lay on the ground, legs hunched beneath him and his head flopped forward on his chest.

★ ★ ★

Hardly daring to breathe, certainly not daring to move, Daniel huddled between the two rocks. There wasn't much room but somehow in desperation he'd pushed himself in between them, hoping he wouldn't get stuck. That was all he needed: to be spotted and be unable to move. From not far away he could hear his pursuers moving about, calling to one another. He thought there were two of them but he didn't dare look to find out.

One of them walked up close to him — he was discovered! — then stopped. Daniel could see the man's legs as he came to a halt right in front of him. All he had to do was turn round and he would see Daniel for sure. Daniel lay as still as he could, aware of sweat on his neck, and wondering if the man would hear the rapid pounding of his heart.

After what seemed like hours he called out, "Can't see him anywhere. Let's go."

"Ain't we goin' to kill the son-ofabitch?"

"I can't stay out here all day, it's too goddamned hot." Forrester was bored with the chase and started to move away. "One's shot, one's on foot. They're dead anyway. And we've got things to do. Perhaps Rex and Pat had better luck than us."

Daniel lay where he was, fearing that maybe their leaving was some sort of trick. Sweat trickled down his face and he was dry mouthed. He blamed both on the heat but inside he knew it was fear.

★ ★ ★

"He ain't here," Rex said in disappointment.

"Then where the hell is he?"

Rex peered down the hill to the canyon far below. "He must have fallen down there, all the way to the bottom."

Pat grinned. "Yeah."

"That makes him dead for sure."

"What about his horse?"

"We'll take it," Rex said but as he reached out for the animal it trotted away from him. Rex swore. He was getting tired of all this, he wanted to go somewhere quiet and think about Clara and her damn cowboy. "Aw, let's leave the goddamned thing. It ain't much of an animal anyhow. But don't tell Pa, he won't be pleased if he finds out." Bruce Forrester always wanted something for nothing.

★ ★ ★

Slowly, cautiously Daniel eased his way out from the two rocks. On trembling legs he walked back to the site of the ambush. No one and nothing disturbed the strong afternoon heat.

"Pemberton! Lee!"

At least there was no sign of Lee's body. At the same time there was no sign of him at all. Where was he? Daniel knew his friend having been shot would need help. He would have to be taken back to Los Santos. But how could Daniel do that? He had no horse, no idea where Los Santos was and, most importantly, no friend.

"Lee!"

He stumbled down the valley calling but getting no reply. Had he been shot again, killed? Please don't let him have been. Movement up on the hill caught his eye and Daniel swung round, his hand going to his gun. He breathed a sigh of relief as he caught a glimpse of Lee's horse.

Daniel climbed the hill, cursing the heat, the Forresters and his own family for sending him away. He spoke to the horse, calming it down, then caught its reins and tied them to a tree. He looked all round, peering over the side of the hill, and came to the same conclusion as Rex and Pat that Lee was in the canyon below. And had to be dead.

All the same he called out, "Lee!" without much hope of an answer and was startled when from not far below him he heard a faint answering cry, "Danny."

"Lee!" Daniel had never been so relieved to hear anyone in his life. "Where are you?"

"Here. Cave."

And by looking closely Daniel too discovered the slash in the hillside. He climbed down to it, pulled away the branches and saw his friend. "Thank God! Here let me help you." He put his arms round Lee pulling him up, wincing as he felt the stickiness of blood. "Can you walk?"

"Yeah," Lee said, trying to grin. "You came for me."

"About time I did," Daniel muttered. "You ain't hurt?"

"No. Don't worry about me."

With Daniel supporting him, Lee managed to climb back to where his horse stood. But by the time they got there, he was unconscious again and didn't look as if he was going to come to.

"And now," Daniel said in some despair, "what the hell am I going to do?"

15

WHILE hunting foxes or shooting grouse, Daniel had often seen people hurt. But they had always been looked after by others while he got on with enjoying himself. He did know that the bullet had to be removed and the wound bound up to stop the bleeding. While he couldn't do anything about the former, he eased Lee's shirt off of him, tearing it into strips and tying them round his body.

What should he do now? Leave Lee here while he rode back to Los Santos to fetch help? No, that would take too long and would mean having to come back into the hills and risk another ambush. While it would take him longer to get to town with Lee, it would in the end prove quicker. That was if he found Los Santos.

And first he had to get Lee on his

horse. Somehow he heaved his friend up, hefted him over his shoulder and with an effort got him into the saddle. Groaning, Lee slumped forward, lying across the animal's neck.

Daniel stood for a moment, getting his breath back, taking deep gulps of air. He had a drink of water, wishing it was whiskey, and wiped the sweat from his face.

In which direction was the town? In some desperation Daniel stared round. They'd ridden out here keeping to a westerly direction, heading deeper into the mountains towards Mexico. It was now early afternoon and the sun was beginning its dip down in the sky. So if he kept the sinking sun behind him he should go in the right direction.

He hoped. With no alternative, Daniel gathered up the horse's reins, and started down the hill. He put one hand on Lee's back to hold him in place, because if he fell off he doubted he'd have enough strength to lift him back up.

* * *

One of the men wore a marshal's badge and the other was dressed like a cowboy. They both looked as if they had come a long way. Clara wondered what they were doing in Los Santos.

"Thank you, Miss," McCullum said as she put two coffees down on the table.

"Is there anything else I can get for you?"

"Some information maybe."

"Oh?"

"Yeah. Have you seen two strangers in town lately? One is an Englishman, young, long dark brown hair." They'd already spoken to Alf Perkins but he'd been unable to help them and McCullum had the feeling that the Town Constable wouldn't be interested in anything except an easy life.

Clara went very red. These two men were after Danny for the murder of that rancher back in Juniper City. But Danny had said he was innocent and while she might not believe him she certainly believed Lee Pemberton, who had vouched for his friend.

Well?"

"Er . . . no . . . I can't say I have." Clara hurried away before she could be asked anything more.

"You believe her?" Craig asked.

McCullum shook his head. "No, she's lying. Wonder why. Not that it matters much. What does matter is that Naughton and his pal have been here. With luck they won't have gone far. Let's have our coffee then start making more inquiries. We'll go over to the saloon, that seems the sort of place Naughton would head for."

★ ★ ★

It was late afternoon when Forrester and his sons rode into the town. People were surprised, and apprehensive, to see them back so soon.

Miguel watched them gallop by, scattering Mexicans, dogs and chickens, not caring if anyone got hurt. What were they here for? What did they want? The boy slipped through the shadows, determined to see what they were up to. He knew he'd be too late to warn Senorita Clara and his sister of their arrival because they'd reach the plaza long before he did but perhaps there would be something he could do.

★ ★ ★

"You know what you've gotta do?" Forrester asked as the gang pulled to a halt by the fountain.

"Yeah, Pa," Dirk said.

Forrester glanced at the windows of the café. Inside he could see Clara and the little Mexican girl she insisted on employing, although Rex had told her not to. There were several customers as well. All innocently going about their business. Couldn't be better. He smiled.

Yelling, "No one hurts my boys!" he drew his rifle.

His sons followed suit.

Someone in the plaza screamed. There were cries and yells. Forrester kicked his horse forward, closely followed by the other three, and the few people in the area scattered for shelter. As the four men galloped by the café, they fired their guns.

Bullets struck the door, the walls, and all the windows shattered in sprays of flying glass.

Clara screamed, dropping the plates she was carrying and they crashed to the floor. She was in the middle of the room in danger of getting shot. Yelling McCullum dived up, flung himself at her, knocking her off her feet, protecting her with his own body.

"Get down!" Craig yelled to the other customers who all fell to the floor, while Conchita ran back into the kitchen, holding her hands over her ears.

Overturning the table he and the Marshal had been sitting at, Craig drew his gun and sent several shots towards the attackers, although he had no real hope of hitting any of them.

They galloped by again. More bullets struck the tables and chairs, smashed into plates and cups.

Suddenly the attack was over as quickly as it had started.

A silence descended over the place, broken only by Conchita's sobbing and someone else's moans.

None too steadily, McCullum helped Clara to her feet and held her as she stared numbly round at the destruction.

"What the hell was all that about?" Craig said, getting up and reloading his gun.

"Is everyone all right?" McCullum called.

"My husband has been hit," a woman said, collapsing down by a man who was holding his arm.

"Conchita?" Clara said shakily.

"I'm all right." The girl emerged from her hiding place, face streaked with tears.

"It was the Forresters," Clara told McCullum and Craig. "The bastards!"

★ ★ ★

Outside Miguel came to an open mouthed halt in the middle of several other citizens, who were slowly emerging onto the plaza, to look at the damage wrought in a few short moments of violence. He couldn't believe what had happened and he started to cry. Poor Senorita Clara. Was she hurt? What about Conchita? Miguel knew he should go and see but with the Forresters still close by he didn't dare leave the safety of the crowd.

The men had gathered a short distance away outside the saloon. They were laughing and whooping, waving their guns in the air.

The door to the courthouse opened and Alf Perkins emerged, strapping on his gun as he came. He paused as he saw the crowd watching Clara, supported by a stranger, coming out of the café. He heard laughing and swung round to face the Forresters. He would have stayed inside if he'd known they were the cause of the trouble but he like everyone else hadn't expected them to come back so soon. He'd imagined he was dealing with a couple of drunken cowboys and that other citizens would help him. Now it was too late to retreat.

"What the hell have you done?" he demanded.

Forrester laughed again. "Shown you good people that when me and mine want something we mean to have it. What you goin' to do about it, old man?"

What he normally did — nothing. Perkins lifted his hands slightly in resignation.

"Sonofabitch coward!" Forrester lifted his rifle and pulled the trigger.

The bullet struck Perkins in the chest. He was slung off his feet, collapsing heavily on the dusty ground, where blood trickled out from the wound.

"Pa!" Rex cried in useless protest.

"Serves him right! Questioning me!"

We'd better get outa here," Dirk

172

said, thinking that maybe even the cowed citizens of Los Santos might take it into their heads to do something to avenge the cold blooded slaying of their constable.

★ ★ ★

It was dark by the time the few lights that shone in Los Santos at night came into view. Weary, footsore Daniel plodded into the town. He'd ridden behind Lee for part of the way but that had made it awkward and uncomfortable for the wounded man so for the most part he'd walked. He was bone tired and scared but his heart lifted a little as he walked towards the plaza. Los Santos might not be much of a place but right then it was a welcome sight, one he had at times not been sure he'd see again.

But something was wrong. The place was quieter than usual. No one was about. Even the saloons were closed up.

What had happened?

Then he saw the shattered windows of the café, the door pock-marked with bullet holes. He came to a halt. What the hell?

Daniel came to the only conclusion he could. The Forresters had done this. They must have ridden back into town right after the ambush.

"Oh God." He urged the horse on. He'd been going to take Lee to Clara as the only friendly face he knew in town and as someone who would know what to do — there was something to be said for independent women after all. Now there was renewed urgency in his steps because if the Forresters had destroyed Clara's café had they also hurt her?

16

"MISS LONG!" Daniel knocked on the girl's door. "Miss Long, are you there?" He could see the faint light of a candle shining through a gap in the shutters. "Clara, please open the door. It's me, Daniel Naughton."

A few moments later Clara stood before him, a shawl wrapped round her nightdress, feet bare.

"Danny!" she exclaimed, then seeing the horse with the body slumped across it, cried out in horror.

And both together they said, "What's happened?"

Daniel added, "Pemberton's been shot. He's badly hurt."

"Oh no!"

"What happened here?"

"Never mind about that now. Let's get Lee inside."

Together they lifted the unconscious man out of the saddle and carried him into Clara's small bedroom. While Daniel supported him, Clara stripped the quilt from the bed and they put him down on the sheet. Clara lit another candle placing it on the chest by the bed.

"Oh my," she breathed.

"He needs help. The bullet is still in him."

"Of course. Danny, you take his horse to the livery while I fetch Doctor Round. Then come back here and sit with me, please."

Daniel nodded and let himself out of the house.

Hastily Clara dressed. Doctor Round lived in one room at the back of the courthouse. He wasn't a very good doctor. He was nearly always either getting drunk or suffering from a hangover. The story went that he used to practise somewhere in the East but had to leave in a hurry when his drunkenness caused the death of a

176

patient. But he was the only doctor Los Santos had. Lee needed him.

Clara knocked on his door, on the window, on the door again until finally shouting, "Hold it a goddamn minute, I'm coming," the doctor answered her summons.

He was still partly dressed in shirt and trousers, braces hanging down round his waist. And what was left of his hair was stuck up on end. As he saw Clara he put his hand behind his back but not before she'd seen the bottle of whiskey he carried in it.

"Clara! What on earth do you want at this time of night? You're not hurt, are you?"

"No but a friend of mine has been shot. Unless the bullet is taken out and his wound properly bandaged he could die."

"Oh . . . but . . . I don't think I can."

"You must." Clara pushed him back inside, taking the bottle from him.

"Hey!"

"You can finish that later." She picked up his coat slung over the back of a chair. "Put that on and find your shoes. You're coming with me."

Doctor Round groaned. "I don't feel up to this."

"Do you want someone else to die because of the Forresters?"

"No. I tried to warn Alf about what would happen. He was going to send for help. He left it too late." Tears came into the man's eyes. "Can't I have a drink for an old friend?"

"Not right now. It would be better for everyone if you sobered up and did what you trained for. Come along, doctor, and quickly!"

Daniel was already back at Clara's house when she and the doctor got there.

"Danny, make some coffee, strong and black. The doctor needs help." Clara ushered Round into the bedroom.

A little while later Clara joined Daniel at the table where he was also drinking coffee. Clara went into the kitchen and came back with some whiskey. She poured a generous amount in Daniel's mug and poured more out for herself. If Daniel was surprised at a girl drinking whiskey so openly, he didn't say so.

"Is the doctor going to cope?"

"He'll have to. There's no one else. What happened? How did Lee get shot?"

"The Forresters ambushed us. I was thrown from my horse and Lee was wounded." To Daniel's relief Clara didn't ask him any more. He was still ashamed for running away and hiding, leaving Lee to his fate. "What about here? I passed your café and saw all the damage."

"That was the Forresters too. I suppose it was some sort of punishment for my refusing Rex. It would be the sort of thing they'd do. But, Danny, that's not the worst of it."

"No?"

"No. My café can be patched up. Bruce Forrester killed Mr Perkins, you know our Constable. He was just standing there, he presented no threat at all, and Forrester shot him down."

"My God! Why?"

"He felt like it I suppose."

"Didn't anyone do anything?"

"It all happened so quickly no one had time to react before the Forresters had ridden out of town. Oh, Danny, it was awful! Poor Mr Perkins. I know he wasn't much of a man and he certainly wasn't much of a constable but he didn't deserve to be shot for no reason whatsoever." And Clara put her head in her hands and began to cry.

Daniel didn't know what to do. He had grown up in a family where feelings were kept under control and he suffered from always having been told to keep a stiff upper lip. Now he felt embarrassed, not used to seeing someone display their emotions so openly. But Clara needed comfort so awkwardly he put out a hand, patting her arm, until her tears subsided.

"I know it's a dreadful thing but maybe Mr Perkins' death will solve Los Santos's problems."

"What do you mean?"

"Well surely the Forresters won't dare come back here now."

Clara frowned. "I don't know. I can't see them leaving their place in the hills, not forever. They might go away for a while but I bet they'll be back. They might not even think the killing warrants them leaving." She paused. "But, Danny, someone's arrived in town who might be willing to do something about them."

Daniel wasn't sure he liked the way she looked at him. What was she talking about? Before she could say any more the bedroom door opened and Round came out. He was wiping his hands on a towel and looked a lot more sober than he had before.

Clara immediately got to her feet and went over to him. "How is he?"

"He's still unconscious. But I've got the bullet out and thanks to his friend there," Round nodded at Daniel, "he hasn't lost a fatal amount of blood. Good job you bandaged him up and got him back here as soon as you did. He's young, healthy." The doctor shrugged. "More than that I can't say. It's up to him and God. Keep him warm and comfortable, Clara. I'll call in tomorrow morning."

"Thank you, doctor."

As soon as he'd gone, Daniel turned back to Clara. "Miss Long, what did you mean? Who's here?"

"Danny, it's two men. They're looking for you. One of them is Marshal McCullum and the other is a young cowboy called Craig Weaver."

"What!" Daniel sank down into the chair. "Oh shit. Oh, I say, Miss Long, I'm sorry. I thought I'd left them way behind."

"Well you haven't. They were in the café when the Forresters shot it up. Marshal McCullum wasn't very pleased about that. He was even unhappier at Mr Perkins' murder. He didn't say a great deal but from what he did say he's determined to go after the gang."

"On his own?" McCullum hadn't struck Daniel as that much of a fool.

"Well, yes, I suppose so. Except for Craig Weaver. And you too I thought."

Daniel took no notice of that, saying, "Perhaps I can slip out of town while they do so."

"Oh, Danny," Clara sighed sadly. "You mean you'd let them go on their own? You wouldn't help them?"

"McCullum wants to arrest me. Weaver wants to shoot me. I have no wish to be taken back to Juniper City to face a lynchmob." More importantly, Daniel didn't want to go after the Forresters again; once was enough.

Clara looked at him as if he'd disappointed her; as, he thought dismally, he seemed to disappoint a lot of people these days. "But Marshal McCullum wouldn't be here in the first place if it wasn't for you."

"He's a lawman. He's paid to take risks."

"And, Danny, don't you see you've now got the chance to tell him what really happened . . . "

"I did that once and he didn't believe me. He beat me up."

"He'll believe you now he knows that the four men exist and what they're capable of. It's your opportunity to prove your innocence. Perhaps your only one. If you run again then whatever you say, whatever anyone else says on your behalf, the Marshal will never believe you."

Daniel sighed heavily. Clara would obviously continue nagging him until he gave in. The worst of it was she was probably right. Why did he have to be involved with an uppity woman who didn't know her place?

From the bedroom they heard Lee groan and Clara, closely followed by Daniel, hurried in to make sure he was all right. He looked peaceful enough, asleep rather than unconscious, his wound neatly and cleanly bandaged. Clara reached out a hand stroking his hair away from his forehead.

"I hope he'll be all right."

"So do I."

"You were brave to bring him back. You saved his life."

Daniel said nothing to that.

"The Marshal is at the hotel, you'd better stay here tonight. You can sleep in the chair. I'll go in the other room."

"All right."

"And, tomorrow, will you go to see Marshal McCullum?"

Daniel sighed again. What choice did he have? "Yes."

"Good. I'm sure it'll turn out for the best."

Daniel wished he could share her optimism.

17

"DANNY. Danny."

The voice woke Daniel and he shifted from his uncomfortable position in the chair. For a moment he wondered where he was and why he had a crick in his neck and one of his arms was numb, coming back to life with painful pins and needles. It was early morning. He could tell that by the shaft of pale light seeping in through the shutters and lying across the floor.

"Danny, you OK?"

It was Lee. He was awake.

Daniel got up and walked over to the bed, sitting on the edge. "Pemberton, old boy! You all right yourself?"

"I've felt better. What happened?"

"You were shot . . . "

"Yeah and then I hid in some sort of cave. I don't remember much after that. Where am I?"

"At Clara's house."

"What in Los Santos? How did I get here? Did you bring me?"

"Yes."

"Well hey then I owe you my life."

"No, I . . . "

"Sure I do. I'd have bled to death out there. You saved me."

"Don't say that."

"What's the matter? Why so gloomy?"

"Oh, Pemberton, Lee, I left you to face those men on your own. I ran away."

The young man stared at Daniel with a puzzled expression on his face. "No, you didn't. You came after me when I was in the cave, I remember that, and afterwards you brought me here."

"I don't mean that."

"What are you talking about?"

"I mean when you were shot. I was scared."

"So was I."

"Too scared to think of anything except myself and escaping. I ran off and hid amongst the rocks."

"You did the right thing."

"You wouldn't have done that. You'd have stayed by me and made sure I was all right."

Lee pulled himself up a bit higher on the pillow. "You couldn't possibly have taken the Forresters on all by yourself. Believe me, my only thought was to get away too."

"I should have done something."

"Danny, what could you have done? You didn't have a horse. Mine galloped away. You couldn't have chased after me."

"They might have caught up with you and killed you."

"They might have done the same to you. They would have done if you hadn't hid. It was a chance we knew we were taking when we went out there. Anyway they didn't succeed."

"Then you're not angry with me?"

"Of course not."

"And you forgive me?"

Lee laughed. "Only if you continue to

call me Lee and don't go back to calling me Pemberton. Danny, honestly, there ain't nothing to forgive."

Daniel sat back, a relieved smile on his face. He still thought he'd acted in a cowardly way but if Lee didn't, then perhaps no one else would either. The trouble was he didn't think he'd behave any differently in the future.

The door opened and Clara came in. "I heard voices. How are you feeling, Lee?"

"Weak, strange. Thirsty."

"I'll get you some water."

"Clara has got a lot to tell you." Daniel stood up. "She'll explain everything."

"Where are you going?"

"Out."

"Why?"

"There's someone I've got to see."

Might as well get it over, Daniel thought. He also thought it might be wise not to wear his gun. If he was unarmed hopefully Marshal McCullum wouldn't be so eager to let anyone shoot him.

The early morning streets were deserted. Alf Perkins was to be buried later that afternoon and the stores were closed for the day as a mark of respect. People were wary of being outside unless their business forced them to, in case the Forresters decided to pay another visit.

With the café in ruins, Marshal McCullum and Craig Weaver were eating breakfast in the hotel and not enjoying the cooking if their faces were anything to go by. Just one other person was in the dining room, sitting in the opposite corner to the lawman and his companion, none of them having chosen to take a table near the windows, just in case.

As Daniel entered the room the two men stared open mouthed at him. Then McCullum exclaimed, "Naughton!" and half stood up, reaching to draw his gun.

Daniel put his hands up. "I'm not armed, Marshal, and I'm not here to make trouble."

"You're giving yourself up!"

"Sort of. Except I haven't done anything to give myself up for."

"So you say!" Craig leapt up, his fists clenched. "Me and Johnny saw you kill Mr Ford."

"But you didn't," Daniel said quickly, hoping that Craig, and the Marshal, would listen to him. "You came across me with his dead body. It's a pity you didn't get there a bit earlier. You'd have seen the four men who did the actual shooting. The same four men who shot up the café yesterday. The same four men anyone in this town will tell you are thieves, cattle rustlers and murderers The Forrester Gang."

Daniel came to a halt and took several deep breaths. His legs were shaking and he badly wanted to sit down. He wondered if either of the men believed him.

McCullum stared at him through narrowed eyes. "Son, perhaps you'd better tell us everything."

"Marshal, no!" Craig protested.

McCullum held out a hand. "You wanna get Mr Ford's killer don't you? You don't want to make a mistake?"

"No, but . . . "

"Then let's hear what Mr Naughton has to say."

"Not here," Daniel said.

"This ain't some sort of trick is it, son? You wouldn't be thinking of doing something foolish like trying to get us alone and shooting us?"

"Of course not," Daniel said indignantly. "There's someone else you should see."

"Your travelling companion?"

"Yes. His employer was killed by the gang. And he's been shot as well."

"My, my, you have had a busy time ain't you? Where is he?"

"At Miss Long's."

"All right then, let's go." And McCullum followed Daniel out of the hotel, a mutinous Craig coming on behind.

"Well, young man," Doctor Round said to Lee, "you're looking a lot better this morning. And so long as you take it easy you'll soon be as good as new."

"I ain't sure I can take it easy, not with the Forresters still free to do what they want."

"Won't do anyone much good if all you succeed in doing is getting hurt some more."

"Doctor Round's right," Clara put in. "Don't worry, Doctor, I won't let him do anything he shouldn't."

Lee made a face but knew when he was beaten, and he really didn't look too unhappy about being told what to do by Clara.

"Looks like you've got company," Doctor Round said as he went out of the door.

"Yes, it's a Marshal from Juniper City."

Marshal McCullum sat back and scratched his head. "This is all a bit difficult to understand." But despite what Daniel thought he wasn't a stupid man. Naughton would hardly have come all this way and ventured into the hills unless he had a good reason.

What else could that reason be, except for what he said: to find Vincent Ford's real killers and prove his own innocence.

"But do you believe me?" Daniel asked anxiously.

"More or less. I'm willing to go along with it for the time being. But, son, if I find out any different you'll be in more trouble than even you could imagine."

"I'll shoot you down," Craig muttered. He still looked unwilling to believe Daniel's story.

"What are you going to do, Marshal?" Lee asked from the bed.

"Go after the Forresters myself. Danny, I presume you want to come as well?"

Daniel didn't, but with everyone looking at him expectantly what else could he do but say yes.

"Me too."

"No, you don't." Clara pushed

194

Lee back down. "You're not going anywhere. You're not well enough. You heard what the Doctor said and what I said to the Doctor."

"But . . ."

"I think someone ought to stay here with Miss Long. Look after her," McCullum said.

"And I'd feel a lot safer with you around," Clara added cunningly.

"I'll need a horse and a gun," Daniel said. "Mine are still in the hills somewhere."

His hopes that that might mean he couldn't go were quickly dashed when McCullum said, "That won't be difficult to arrange. But there is another, more difficult problem. The same one you two had. Where exactly do we find their hide-out?"

"I believe, senor, my brother can help you with that."

They all turned round. Conchita stood in the bedroom doorway with Miguel in front of her, her hands on his shoulders.

"Conchita! How long have you been there?"

"I'm sorry, Clara, the door was open. We came in to see if you was all right and heard voices. We've been listening to what you all say."

"I'm not cross. I was just surprised to see you that's all. What did you mean about Miguel helping the Marshal?"

"The place you seek is near to where our family's sheep farm used to be. Miguel knows where it is. He can guide the lawmen there."

"No!" Clara said at once. "I can't allow it. It might be dangerous."

"I will be very careful, Senorita Clara. I want to help these senors find the Forresters. They are dreadful men, always hurting others. Hurting you. They should be stopped."

"Can't you just tell them how to get there?"

"Si, but is difficult."

"It'd be quicker if he goes with us," McCullum pointed out. "I'd make very sure nothing happened to him," he

196

promised. "As soon as we get near the ranch I'll send him home. I won't let him get anywhere near the Forresters."

"Please, Senorita Clara. Please."

"Oh very well." In her heart Clara still didn't like this but she could think of no objection anyone else was likely to take notice of. "Just so long as you are careful, Miguel."

"I will be, Senorita."

"Let's get ready to go then."

Daniel had to know the answer to one thing before they left and he drew the lawman to one side. "Marshal, back in Juniper City were you going to let a mob lynch me?"

McCullum looked surprised and angry. "Of course I wasn't. What are you talking about?"

"Why did you let Lee Pemberton go? I thought it was so there wouldn't be any witnesses."

"Then you were wrong. It was simply that I thought if I had you in the cells all by yourself it would be easier for you."

"Oh!"

"Now are you ready? Come on."

As McCullum opened the front door and went to step outside in the street, it seemed that the Delgado children weren't the only ones wanting to know what was happening. Gathered in front of Clara's house were several of the townsmen, with Doctor Round standing at their head.

18

"**W**HAT'S the matter?" Clara asked, joining Daniel and the others at the door.

"Nothing," Doctor Round said, a sudden new dignity about him. "It's simply that poor Alf Perkins was shot and killed yesterday because we sat back and did nothing in the past. If we had stood together when the Forresters first came here perhaps they wouldn't have stayed. They certainly wouldn't have ridden roughshod over us as they have. We made things easy for them and now it's time to do something about it. We're ready to ride out with you, Marshal."

"Well, I can't say I wouldn't welcome your help. Let's get our horses and we can be on our way. Miguel, you ride up front with me. And don't worry, Miss Long, Conchita, I'll take real good care of him."

But all the precautions they took
— sending Miguel back to Los Santos
as soon as they were near the hide-
out, then approaching it silently and
carefully — were in vain.

The ranch was deserted.

The posse came to a halt on the ridge
that overlooked it. The hide-out nestled
at the foot of the rocks. The house was
small, a ramshackle affair, part of the
porch broken away, the roof patched
up with tin. Out front was a corral in
which a couple of horses grazed, and
off to one side was a barn, again in
a poor state of repair. A bunkhouse,
where the outlaws who hid out at the
place, slept, was beyond the barn.

Apart from the horses there was no
sign of life about the place: no smoke
coming from the chimneys, no activity
in the barn, not even any cattle in the
meadow.

As they watched, the bunkhouse door
opened and two men hurried out. They

went to the corral, caught and saddled the horses, and rode out at a gallop.

"Let 'em go," McCullum said once Doctor Round had confirmed that neither was a member of the Forrester family. Doubtless they were outlaws wanted by the law but the Marshal didn't have enough men to go up against them as well.

"What do you think's happened?" Daniel asked.

"I reckon the Forresters got cold feet after shooting the Constable. They've decided to hightail it out of here and hide out some place else. For the time being anyway."

"Let's hope we've got rid of them at last," the Doctor said.

"We'd better go down and see if they've left any clue behind as to where they've gone." McCullum didn't really think that was likely but he couldn't leave without looking round. At the least they might find some stolen goods that could be returned to their rightful owners.

"You ain't letting 'em get way with what they've done are you?" Craig Weaver asked anxiously.

"No. Now I want 'em not only for shooting the Constable but for killing Mr Ford as well. Let's go. And I hardly need to remind you all to be careful. Bear in mind this could be some sorta trap."

Just what I needed to know, Daniel thought sourly. He eased his gun in its holster and rode down the rocky slope, trying to keep in the middle of all the others.

* * *

"I wish I could have gone with the posse," Lee Pemberton moaned. "It ain't fair or right that I'm stuck here in bed while they're out there, perhaps in danger." Lee was proving a most difficult patient, wanting Clara to bring him this, that and the other; not liking the inactivity of having to lie in bed.

Clara sighed, trying not to remind

him that that was about the tenth time during the morning that he'd said more or less the same thing. Her reply was almost the same as she'd made before as well. "You've done more than your fair share to bring the gang to justice. And you've been shot. Don't fret you'll soon be up and about. And then you can be on your way back to Texas and the ranch."

But somehow neither Texas nor the ranch where he was foreman held quite the same appeal for Lee as they had done just a few days ago. But before he could tell Clara so she went on.

"Now is there anything else you need?"

"Where are you going?"

"To attend Mr Perkins' funeral. Someone has to. Most of his other friends are out with Marshal McCullum. I won't be long." She bent over and kissed his cheek but before he could do or say anything about that either she was gone.

Gun held ready, Daniel followed McCullum onto the porch and into the house. He wrinkled his nose. He wasn't that fussy — after all the manorhouse in Kent was draughty, cold and inconvenient — but the place was filthy. Dust covered everything. Cobwebs hung in the corners. Dishes were piled up on the table together with stale food. And a mouse scampered into a hole by the fireplace.

"I wonder if it's always like this," he said. "Or because they left in a hurry."

"Somehow I can't imagine the Forresters being particularly concerned about how they live. Look in there, son . . ."

McCullum came to halt as from somewhere outside there was an almighty screech.

"What the hell?"

Reluctantly Daniel went outside with the man, to the accompaniment of more screeches. What could they mean? Like them, the others all arrived to see what the noise was about and watched as Craig Weaver dragged a struggling, screaming woman from the barn out into the open.

"Edith Forrester," Doctor Round confirmed.

As the woman saw the group of men gathered in the yard, she stopped struggling, instead sinking to her knees, sobbing wildly.

"She was hiding under some straw in the barn. She tried to attack me when I found her," Craig explained a bit helplessly.

"It's all right," McCullum said. "Danny, see if you can find the means of making her some coffee while I try and get her calmed down. The rest of you get on with searching."

Daniel went back into the house and into the kitchen which if anything was even dirtier than the rest of the place. More by luck than knowledge he lit the stove and started boiling up some water. He found a couple of reasonably clean cups and spooned coffee into them. Naturally there was no milk or sugar; or any tea. Right then he would have given anything for a nice hot cup of tea but he'd long given up asking for such a thing.

When he took the coffee outside, Edith Forrester was sitting at the table, McCullum and Craig on either side of her. She looked much calmer but still inclined to be tearful and she had a bruise on one cheek and her top lip was split and had bled. Craig hadn't done that, even by accident, they were older, deliberate wounds.

"They left me behind," she was saying. "They've all gone. They left me."

"Do you know where they've gone?" McCullum asked.

Edith shook her head. "Over the border maybe. I think some of the others were taking the cattle to sell in Mexico if they could. Bit of a nerve," she added with a bitter laugh, "seeing as how they stole the cattle from the Mexicans in the first place."

"Your husband . . . "

"I tell you I don't know! Bruce didn't say what he was going to do. He could be going into Arizona. He does sometimes. I don't know." And she began to cry again.

Daniel put the coffee down in front of her. She gulped, mumbled something, gulped again and picked up the cup, holding it with both hands as if she was cold and wanted to warm herself.

McCullum said gently, "You know why they've gone, don't you?"

Edith drank some coffee then nodded. "I couldn't believe it when I heard what they'd done. Of all the senseless things."

"You could say that," Craig said. "Most of their murders have been done without quite so many witnesses."

"Hush," McCullum told him, not wanting to start Edith crying again. "Did your husband do that to you?" he indicated the bruises and the blood.

She nodded.

"And I bet that ain't the first time either. But why now? Was it just because he was angry over what had happened?"

"No."

"Then why? Why has he left you behind?"

"Because I tried to stop Rex."

Daniel went cold inside with a sudden frightening premonition. "Stop Rex from doing what?"

"He was going to join his Pa and the others later. He had something to do first."

The premonition grew stronger.

"He's going into Los Santos after Clara Long. What he means to do to that nice little girl is wrong, wrong, wrong!"

"Oh no." Daniel looked at McCullum and Craig in dismay. They had played into Rex Forrester's hands. While they were here at the hide-out, Clara and a badly wounded Lee were all alone. "What are we going to do?"

19

ALF PERKINS was buried in the cemetery at the rear of the Mexican Catholic Church, the service conducted by the Mexican priest. No one knew if he had been a Catholic or not but as it was Los Santos's only church and the priest its only priest, there really was no alternative.

Clara and Conchita sat together during the service. Quite a few other people attended — the men who hadn't gone with the posse, the town's few other respectable women, even some of the not so respectable women, for Mr Perkins had been a good friend to them, always ignoring their activities in exchange for money.

The congregation was there not just because of Mr Perkins; Clara knew it was because everyone was angry and upset at the way in which he had died. They wanted to show a united front against the Forresters.

Afterwards they all went outside and stood under the hot sun while the coffin was lowered into the ground.

"Thank you for coming," the priest said when the service was over. "Let us hope more deaths will not be necessary."

"Or at least no more innocent deaths," someone near to Clara muttered. "Damn Forresters."

"Conchita, come home with me," Clara said as they left the graveyard. "Have something to eat." She knew that the girl was worried about Miguel and didn't want her to be alone. "We can wait together."

"Si, Clara, I would like that. I wonder when the others will be back."

"Not before dark I shouldn't imagine."

"I hope everything is all right."

"I'm sure it will be. Marshal McCullum seemed a very experienced lawman. He'll know what to do."

"What we'd better do is get back to Los Santos and pretty damn quick too." Marshal McCullum lumbered to his feet.

"We'll be too late."

"What are we going to do with her?" Craig indicated Edith Forrester, who was crying once more.

"We can't leave her here, not all by herself. We'll have to take her back into town with us."

"She'll slow us up," Daniel pointed out.

McCullum realized that the young man was right. Not that Edith would do so on purpose but she was so distraught that even now Craig was having difficulty in persuading her to stand up. God only knew how she'd get on a horse let alone ride it. "OK, us three will ride on ahead of the others. She can follow with that doctor fellow."

Had Daniel not been so anxious

about Lee, and Clara, he might have considered the dangers of riding back to Los Santos with just McCullum and Craig Weaver, and decided instead to stay with the larger number of men, at the rear, where it was safe. As it was he didn't even think of that until it was too late and he was on his horse, galloping along by McCullum's side, facing any possible trouble from the front.

"Oh bloody hell," he muttered but couldn't come up with a good enough excuse to turn round and go back.

★ ★ ★

Lee Pemberton sulked in bed. What was happening? Where was Clara? He wanted a drink of water. She should be back by now. Had the posse caught up with, killed, the Forresters? He didn't like this doing nothing, waiting. He shouldn't have listened to the doctor, to Danny or to Clara. He should have gone with them.

From the other room he thought he heard a small sound, like that of one of the shutters being pushed open. Was it Clara returning? He listened hard. But hearing nothing more, came to the conclusion he'd been mistaken and lay back in the bed, closing his eyes.

* * *

Almost as soon as Clara opened the door she realized something was wrong. The shutters she had left almost closed were now fully open. Lee had no reason to do that . . .

"Conchita," she said to the girl who was close behind her, then Rex Forrester stepped out from behind the door.

He punched Conchita hard round the side of her face. Without even a moan the girl collapsed to the floor, crumpled in a heap on her stomach. "Damn Mexican whore!" Rex snarled and kicked out at her.

"Don't!" Clara cried in a horrified tone. "Stop it!"

"Shut up!" Rex said and caught hold of a handful of the girl's hair, pulling her further into the room, slamming the door shut.

Clara was terrified. No one was around to see what had happened. She was now shut up in her own house with this dreadful man. She was scared for herself but she was even more scared for Lee. Did Rex know Lee was in the bedroom, wounded? Had he already gone in there and finished off what had been started in the hills?

"Let me go," she protested as Rex dragged her towards the bedroom door. Tears came into her eyes as he tugged at her hair. She reached out trying to stop him but he knocked her hand away and ignored her struggles and kicks. She knew he was much too strong for her and she would never get away from him. Her only hope was Lee, but supposing Lee was dead? Clara didn't think she could bear it if he was. "You're hurting."

Rex opened the bedroom door and threw her through it so hard she bounced off the bed and fell to the floor. Rex followed with a smirk on his face then came to a halt as he saw Lee scrambling out of the far side of the bed, reaching for the gun on the chest of drawers.

Clara's heart lightened. Lee was alive!

"Hey!" Rex shouted. "What the hell! You two timing little whore!"

"Don't do anything foolish," Lee said, picking up the gun. "Are you all right, Clara?"

"Yes," the girl said shakily, scrambling to her feet.

"Goddammit!" Rex shouted. "She's my girl!" And his hand went towards his holstered gun. "You ain't getting away with it this time."

"Don't," Lee warned. He brought his gun up, pointing it at the young man. But Rex's eyes had the light of madness glinting in them and Lee knew he wasn't about to listen to reason.

"Rex, no, don't!" Clara cried.

"I'm goin' to kill you both!"

Rex's hand enclosed round his gun, pulling it out of the holster. Both Lee and Clara yelled at him to stop but he took no notice. He was quick too and his finger was already tightening on the trigger before Lee fired.

The bullet struck Rex near to the heart. A look of surprised panic came over his face. He hit the wall and slid slowly down it to come to rest in a sitting position with his legs stuck out in front of him.

"Clara," he said reaching out a hand towards her. "I meant you no harm. I love you."

Even as she hurried over to him his eyes glazed over and his head flopped to one side.

"He's dead," Lee said dropping his gun on the bed and taking Clara in his arms.

20

"**W**HERE the hell is he?" Bruce Forrester strode up and down the untidy campsite, his face lit up by the flames of the fire. "He should be back by now. He knew I wanted to be on my way to Mexico."

"Perhaps the girl is proving difficult," Dirk suggested.

"Then he'll have to leave her behind. Our lives are more important than a girl. He can have all the goddamn girls he wants once we get to Mexico."

Dirk and Pat glanced at one another. They both knew their father had realized he'd gone too far in gunning down Alf Perkins and he wanted to get away before the law came for him. If it had been other than his youngest, and favourite, son he wouldn't have delayed this long.

"Dirk, you go on into Los Santos, find out what's happened."

"OK, Pa." Dirk got up with a sigh. Why was it always him who had to sort out his youngest brother's mistakes?

"Be as quick as you can. And be sure to bring Rex back with you."

★ ★ ★

As Daniel, McCullum and Craig rode up, the undertaker's black hearse was just pulling away from Clara's.

"Oh bloody hell, we're too late."

But almost immediately Clara ran out calling, "It's all right. We're all right."

"Who's dead?" McCullum demanded.

"Rex Forrester. Come in and I'll explain."

As the men dismounted Conchita appeared in the doorway. A bruise had already formed on her cheek from Rex's blow and one of her front teeth was knocked loose. She twisted her hands together, looking worried. "Senor,

218

where is Miguel. Isn't he with you?"

"Isn't he here?" McCullum frowned at the others.

"No."

"He should be."

Even if Miguel hadn't ridden as fast as they had, he should have arrived back by now. It was unlikely he'd got lost, seeing as how he was the one who had taken them to the hide-out. Had he fallen off the horse, been hurt? Or had something worse happened? At the time it had seemed sensible to send him back by himself, so that he wasn't exposed to any danger at the Forresters' place. Now it didn't seem sensible at all.

"Please," Conchita said, "he must be all right. He cannot have done anything foolish. Oh, but he can be so headstrong."

"Is there anyone else he would have gone to see? Someone he'd boast to about his exploits?"

"No, no. He would know I'd be worried about him and come back here. Something bad has happened to him." And Conchita began to cry.

"I'm sure he'll be all right," Clara said, putting her arm round the girl. But she was just as worried as Conchita. She should have put her foot down and refused to let Miguel go. If anything had happened to him she would never forgive herself. "Come along, Conchita, let's get supper ready. Miguel will be back for that."

Conchita gave a weak smile.

"I hope he turns up soon," McCullum said, chewing his lip. Where was the boy? Why wasn't he back?

* * *

"What happens now?" Lee asked Marshal McCullum. "I ain't sure. Once Forrester hears about the death of his son he won't take it lightly. But whether or not he comes straight back here to exact revenge or waits until he hopes his killing of Perkins has been forgotten, I don't know."

"It wasn't Lee's fault," Clara said. "Rex gave him no choice."

"I ain't saying it is. And, quite frankly, I can't say it grieves me much that someone like Rex Forrester is dead. What I am saying is that his father ain't the type to forgive or forget. There's Miguel as well. We've got to find him."

"Maybe we ought to go after Forrester before he comes after us," Craig suggested.

Daniel hid a sigh. He'd been afraid someone would suggest something foolish like that. That was the trouble with these Westerners — they were so rash.

"Might be best at that," Lee agreed.

— Rash — all of them

"I don't really want to spend the rest of my life looking over my shoulder to see if Forrester and his two sons are coming up behind me."

"We can't do anything if they've gone to Mexico." Daniel tried to instil some sense into the proceedings. Trouble was no one took any notice of him.

"And I don't intend to leave Los Santos," Clara stated. "My home is here. I'm not running away."

"Then we do something about them before they do anything to us." Craig sat back looking pleased. "Good!"

Daniel wondered if he could say it was no longer his fight. His name had been cleared. He was free to go. He wanted to go. All the same he kept quiet. He might not mind knowing he was a coward but he didn't want everyone else knowing as well.

"Where's Edith?" Clara asked.

"Once they got back here, Doc Round was going to take her to the hotel," McCullum replied.

"I feel sorry for her. It wasn't her fault she had such a terrible family and it can't have been easy for her living with them. She must have been so scared all the time."

Lee caught hold of her hand and squeezed it. Clara smiled.

"So we start out tomorrow?" Craig said.

"Yeah I don't see why not."

★ ★ ★

Forrester raised clenched fists towards the dark sky and opened his mouth in an anguished yell.

Rex was dead. Shot by that goddamn cowboy and all over a girl, who was no better than a whore, having the cowboy in her bed. Well they would all pay! Cowboy, girl and town! He'd make them pay! All thought of escaping to Mexico fled his mind. No one hurt his family and got away with it. He wanted — would have — revenge.

"What are we going to do now, Pa?" Dirk asked. As far as he and Pat were concerned their brother had no one but himself to blame. They were sorry he was dead but their own lives were far more important.

"We go back to Los Santos and we kill that goddamned sonofabitch and

223

the whore too! And anyone else who gets in our way!"

"But, Pa, I thought we were going to Mexico," Pat protested.

Forrester strode angrily over to his son and caught hold of his jacket collar, almost strangling him with his tight grip. "You want me to leave, now?" he yelled. "You expect me to run away and leave unpunished those responsible for Rex's murder? You expect me to do nothing?"

"Pat didn't mean that, Pa."

"I'll have revenge for my son and if you were a proper child of mine you'd want revenge for your brother. You goddamned coward!" Forrester flung Pat from him so he almost fell.

Sulkily, Pat rubbed his neck. "All I meant was, is it safe right now with the law looking for us an' all?"

"Oh, I think it'll be safe enough, don't you, when we've got us a hostage." And grinning Forrester went over to where Miguel cringed by the horses' legs.

The boy's ankles were tied together, his hands tied behind his back. Blood trickled from his mouth and nose and one eye was blackened, almost closed. Tears had left tracks down his cheeks.

"I knew a little Mex bastard would come in handy one day," Forrester went on, jerking the boy to his feet. "I never expected it to be so soon nor over a goddamned cowboy and a whore."

Miguel could feel himself close to crying again. They were going to kill Senorita Clara and there was not only nothing he could do about it, they had it in mind that he was going to help them.

* * *

Daniel woke up early, moaning as he tried to ease the ache in his neck and back from sleeping yet another night in the chair in Clara's bedroom.

They had all sat up long into the evening discussing what might be done and who in Los Santos they could continue to rely on for help. Conchita became more and more agitated about her brother so that in the end while McCullum and Craig went back to their room at the hotel, Clara had asked the girl to stay with her, an offer Conchita gladly accepted. They'd slept on the floor in the other room.

Daniel thought that maybe he could sneak away during the night, leave the others to get on with their troubles. But despite the fact that the chair was so uncomfortable he'd fallen asleep straightaway and hadn't woken up again until now, when it was too late. He stretched and stood up. At the same time Lee opened his eyes.

"How are you feeling, old boy?"

"Well enough that this time when you go after the Forresters I won't be left behind."

Daniel smiled weakly. Why so eager to rush into danger? Why so foolish?

"I'll go and see if Miss Long and . . . " he began but got no further as several shots rang out from the direction of the plaza. "What the hell!"

There were more shots. Then a voice demanded, "Clara Long! Pemberton! Come on out and collect your just desserts!"

"My God!" Lee exclaimed. "That's Forrester!"

"Or, by Christ, the kid gets it instead!"

And this was followed by a high pitched squeal of pain.

"And that's Miguel!" Daniel added.

21

BRUCE FORRESTER stood at one end of the plaza, one arm round Miguel's throat, holding him tightly in front of him. The boy looked hurt and terrified. Pat Forrester stood nearby. They both had guns out, held ready to fire. Of the eldest brother, Dirk, there was no sign.

"Be careful, Danny," Lee said as they entered the plaza from the other end, hiding round the corner of the hotel, out of the line of fire. "He's bound to be around somewhere."

"Miguel!" Conchita cried as she saw her brother and would have run to him had Clara not caught hold of her arm and stopped her.

McCullum and Craig had emerged from the hotel and Doctor Round and several of the townsmen were standing watching.

"Stay where you are, all of you!" Forrester yelled. "Or the kid here gets hurt. You all know I will hurt him, him bein' only a Mexican. Now all we want is the goddamn murderer who shot down my poor boy in cold blood . . ."

"He asked for it," Lee muttered but didn't say so to Forrester, believing the man wouldn't appreciate it.

" . . . and Miss Long who was responsible for what happened by two timing Rex."

"Oh really, he's as ridiculous as Rex was," Clara said crossly.

"Bruce, no!" Edith cried from where she stood in the hotel doorway.

"Get inside, woman. This ain't nothin' to do with you or don't you care your son got shot?"

"Best do as he says," McCullum told her.

"Isn't there anything we can do?" Craig asked, unable to keep still in his frustration.

"Dammit I don't see what. The

bastard is holding all the cards. But, Craig, watch out for any chance to kill him and his goddamned sons."

"Sure thing, Marshal."

Forrester called across the plaza. "You hand those two over to me for punishment and I'll not only let the kid here go nice and safe and sound but I promise me and my boys will go away and leave you in peace. We ain't got no quarrel with Los Santos."

"Do you believe him?" Daniel asked.

Lee shook his head. "But it doesn't matter whether I do or not. There's no way I'm letting them get their hands on Clara."

"What are we going to do then?"

"I'll give you a minute or two to think about it then we start hurting the kid."

"Oh no!" Conchita wept. "Please, senors, you must do something. Don't let them hurt Miguel."

"They won't do anything," Daniel said. "He's just a boy."

"You heard what that man said. He's

a Mexican boy," Conchita sobbed. "His life means nothing to them."

"She's right," Lee agreed. "Looks like I'll have to give myself up."

"Lee, you can't!"

"I won't let you," Clara added. "They'll kill you."

"I can't let Miguel be hurt because of me."

Daniel marvelled at his friend. "There's no way I'd sacrifice myself for someone else."

"Yeah, you would."

"No, I wouldn't."

"For goodness sake!" Clara interrupted. "We haven't got time for you two to start arguing again."

"Sorry," Lee said. "Keep your eyes open. I'm going."

"Don't!" Clara clutched at his arm.

He shrugged her off and stepped out into the open. "Hey, Forrester! Here I am. Now you can let go of Miguel."

"Be careful," McCullum muttered.

The man swung round to look at Lee. He raised his gun and for a moment Daniel thought he was going to shoot but he didn't. Instead smiling in a nasty way, he said, "Take your weapon out of the holster and put it on the ground. Slowly! That's right. Walk on over to me."

"Let the boy go first."

"You ain't in no position to make demands." And Forrester did something to Miguel that made him cry out in pain.

Daniel glanced across at McCullum and Craig. Both looked as helpless and as angry as he felt.

"Where's the bitch?"

"You can't expect anyone to agree to handing her over to you. You'll have to make do with me. Anyway she didn't shoot Rex, I did, and a pleasure it was too. Your quarrel is with me."

"I don't know about that."

"I'm all you're getting."

"Step on over here and we can discuss that some more."

"We must do something," Clara said.

"Yes, but what? Forrester has the upper hand. What I'd like to know is where Dirk is?"

"Right behind you," a voice said in his ear.

Clara squealed in fright and Daniel felt his heart leap from his chest into his mouth as the hard barrel of a gun was stuck in his back.

"Jesus," he breathed.

"Don't try anything," Dirk ordered. "I don't know who you are but you're in the way." He shoved Daniel away hard, kicking his legs out from under him so that Daniel fell to the ground and at the same time grabbed hold of Clara's arm, pulling her close to him, digging the gun into her side. "I've got her, Pa!"

"No!" Lee came to a startled halt. What had happened?

Helped by Conchita, Daniel scrambled up, and found himself with Dirk's gun pointed back at him. "Perhaps you'd better come on out to join Pa as well. You seem to have something to do with this. You too, little girl." And still holding Clara he herded them all out into the plaza, towards the guns and baleful eyes of Forrester and Pat.

Please let someone do something, Daniel thought. What am I doing here about to get shot by a mad man and his mad sons? Doubtless his father would be most displeased to learn that his son had met his end in a shoot out on the dusty street of a small New Mexican town. Displeased, disappointed — but probably not surprised.

"Well, well," Forrester said. "All my favourite people in one place."

Clara said, "Conchita and Miguel are nothing to do with this."

"They're Mexes and they used to work for you despite Rex telling you he didn't like it," Forrester said and suddenly, just like that, he shot Miguel.

"My God!" Craig said appalled and would have pulled out his gun had not McCullum stopped him.

"There's too many people in the way."

The boy's cry as he dropped to the ground was echoed by the screams of Clara and Conchita. Conchita ran up to her brother, flinging herself down in the dust beside him, cradling his head in her arms, sobbing.

"You bastard," Lee said. For the moment Forrester had no hostage to protect him. That wouldn't last long. He was already reaching for Clara. If he got hold of her they'd never be able to do anything. They would, eventually, be killed. They might as well go out fighting as well as submit meekly to whatever the man had in mind. Lee took his chance. He leapt at Forrester.

"Look out, Pa!" Dirk yelled.

Lee and Forrester sprawled on the ground. Forrester lost his grip on his gun and quickly Daniel kicked it towards Lee, who grasped it, jammed it against the man's body and pulled the trigger. Twice. Screaming in shock, Forrester rolled away, clutching at the wounds in his chest.

As Dirk cried out "No!" Clara kicked him hard on his ankle. With a little yelp of pain he loosened his grip on her arm and she flung herself at Conchita and Miguel, hugging them both.

Pat shot at Lee, who was just getting up, missed, then turned, pushed by Daniel, and ran away. Only into the arms of McCullum and Craig who wrestled him to the ground.

Yelling, Dirk fired at both Lee and Daniel. At the same time, he dodged backwards across the plaza.

Hardly knowing what he was doing, Daniel dragged his gun from its holster, aimed carefully and fired. He was a good shot. The bullet smashed Dirk in the throat. At the same time shots from Doctor Round and Marshal McCullum also hit him. Dirk jerked sidewards, his legs struck the side of the fountain and he fell in, sending a spray of water high up in the air.

The plaza fell silent.

Slowly Clara helped Conchita up and they both knelt over Miguel,

Doctor Round already approaching to see what he could do. McCullum and Craig, holding a dispirited Pat Forrester between them, hurried over. And Edith Forrester again came to the hotel doorway, hand to her mouth, eyes wide with shock.

And Lee turned to Daniel. He didn't know much about England but he was quite sure they didn't have gun fights in the street there and he was also sure that Daniel had never before killed anyone. He didn't know how his friend would react. "Are you all right?"

"Of course I am. Bit like potting a pheasant as a matter of a fact." But despite his arrogant tone, Daniel's knees suddenly gave way and he clamped down on the sickness rising in his throat. "Oh, Lee, I've just killed a man."

"The bastard needed killing. It's the way it is sometimes."

"Yes I know. But right now that doesn't make it any easier. What on earth will my father say when he finds out?"

★ ★ ★

Los Santos was back to its peaceful, lazy self.

Marshal McCullum and Craig Weaver had left for Juniper City, along with Pat Forrester as their prisoner, and Edith, who had nowhere to go and no one to be with, except for her arrested son.

Miguel wasn't badly wounded and was basking in being fussed over by Clara and Conchita. He had the feeling it wasn't going to last long and it would soon be back to normal. Doctor Round was also organising the townsmen to repair the café.

"After all," he said, "we need somewhere to get a decent meal. And Los Santos owes you, Clara."

And Lee told Daniel he was going to stay with Clara.

"Why aren't I surprised?" Daniel said, smiling.

"I've been a cowboy for a long while, it's time I had a change and this place, I mean both the café and the town, has potential for growth. Maybe I can even become Town Constable."

"But most of all you want to stay because you love Clara."

Lee reddened. "Yeah."

"Jolly good. Despite the fact that she's still much too independent for me, she's a nice girl, and I'm sure you'll be very happy."

"Thanks. Danny, will you stay with us? There's plenty to do. We could use your help."

Daniel was tempted. But not for long. He wanted to move on. "I appreciate your offer, old boy, but there's a silver strike over in Arizona, which is where I was on my way to before all this started. I've still a mind to go there. If I'm lucky I'll find enough silver so that I can return to England a rich man and show them all how well I've done."

★ ★ ★

As Lee and Clara watched Daniel ride away, Clara said, "Do you think that's likely?"

And Lee replied," No, not in the least."

THE END

FIGHTING RAMROD
Charles N. Heckelmann

Most men would have cut their losses, but Frazer counted the bullets in his guns and said he'd soak the range in blood before he'd give up another inch of what was his.

LONE GUN
Eric Allen

Smoke Blackbird had been away too long. The Lequires had seized the Blackbird farm, forcing the Indians and settlers off, and no one seemed willing to fight! He had to fight alone.

THE THIRD RIDER
Barry Cord

Mel Rawlins wasn't going to let anything stand in his way. His father was murdered, his two brothers gone. Now Mel rode for vengeance.

ARIZONA DRIFTERS
W. C. Tuttle

When drifting Dutton and Lonnie Steelman decide to become partners they find that they have a common enemy in the formidable Thurston brothers.

TOMBSTONE
Matt Braun

Wells Fargo paid Luke Starbuck to outgun the silver-thieving stagecoach gang at Tombstone. Before long Luke can see the only thing bearing fruit in this eldorado will be the gallows tree.

HIGH BORDER RIDERS
Lee Floren

Buckshot McKee and Tortilla Joe cut the trail of a border tough who was running Mexican beef into Texas. They stopped the smuggler in his tracks.

BRETT RANDALL, GAMBLER
E. B. Mann

Larry Day had the choice of running away from the law or of assuming a dead man's place. No matter what he decided he was bound to end up dead.

THE GUNSHARP
William R. Cox

The Eggerleys weren't very smart. They trained their sights on Will Carney and Arizona's biggest blood bath began.

THE DEPUTY OF SAN RIANO
Lawrence A. Keating and
Al. P. Nelson

When a man fell dead from his horse, Ed Grant was spotted riding away from the scene. The deputy sheriff rode out after him and came up against everything from gunfire to dynamite.

FARGO: MASSACRE RIVER
John Benteen

The ambushers up ahead had now blocked the road. Fargo's convoy was a jumble, a perfect target for the insurgents' weapons!

SUNDANCE: DEATH IN THE LAVA
John Benteen

The Modoc's captured the wagon train and its cargo of gold. But now the halfbreed they called Sundance was going after it . . .

HARSH RECKONING
Phil Ketchum

Five years of keeping himself alive in a brutal prison had made Brand tough and careless about who he gunned down . . .

FARGO: PANAMA GOLD
John Benteen

With foreign money behind him, Buckner was going to destroy the Panama Canal before it could be completed. Fargo's job was to stop Buckner.

FARGO:
THE SHARPSHOOTERS
John Benteen

The Canfield clan, thirty strong were raising hell in Texas. Fargo was tough enough to hold his own against the whole clan.

PISTOL LAW
Paul Evan Lehman

Lance Jones came back to Mustang for just one thing — revenge! Revenge on the people who had him thrown in jail.

HELL RIDERS
Steve Mensing

Wade Walker's kid brother, Duane, was locked up in the Silver City jail facing a rope at dawn. Wade was a ruthless outlaw, but he was smart, and he had vowed to have his brother out of jail before morning!

DESERT OF THE DAMNED
Nelson Nye

The law was after him for the murder of a marshal — a murder he didn't commit. Breen was after him for revenge — and Breen wouldn't stop at anything . . . blackmail, a frameup . . . or murder.

DAY OF THE COMANCHEROS
Steven C. Lawrence

Their very name struck terror into men's hearts — the Comancheros, a savage army of cutthroats who swept across Texas, leaving behind a bloodstained trail of robbery and murder.

SUNDANCE: SILENT ENEMY
John Benteen

A lone crazed Cheyenne was on a personal war path. They needed to pit one man against one crazed Indian. That man was Sundance.

LASSITER
Jack Slade

Lassiter wasn't the kind of man to listen to reason. Cross him once and he'll hold a grudge for years to come — if he let you live that long.

LAST STAGE TO GOMORRAH
Barry Cord

Jeff Carter, tough ex-riverboat gambler, now had himself a horse ranch that kept him free from gunfights and card games. Until Sturvesant of Wells Fargo showed up.

McALLISTER ON THE COMANCHE CROSSING
Matt Chisholm

The Comanche, McAllister owes them a life — and the trail is soaked with the blood of the men who had tried to outrun them before.

QUICK-TRIGGER COUNTRY
Clem Colt

Turkey Red hooked up with Curly Bill Graham's outlaw crew. But wholesale murder was out of Turk's line, so when range war flared he bucked the whole border gang alone . . .

CAMPAIGNING
Jim Miller

Ambushed on the Santa Fe trail, Sean Callahan is saved by two Indian strangers. But there'll be more lead and arrows flying before the band join Kit Carson against the Comanches.

GUNSLINGER'S RANGE
Jackson Cole

Three escaped convicts are out for revenge. They won't rest until they put a bullet through the head of the dirty snake who locked them behind bars.

RUSTLER'S TRAIL
Lee Floren

Jim Carlin knew he would have to stand up and fight because he had staked his claim right in the middle of Big Ike Outland's best grass.

THE TRUTH ABOUT SNAKE RIDGE
Marshall Grover

The troubleshooters came to San Cristobal to help the needy. For Larry and Stretch the turmoil began with a brawl and then an ambush.